Confessions of a Gangsta

Lock Down Publications & Ca$h
Presents
Confessions of a Gangsta
A Novel by *Nicholas Lock*

Confessions of a Gangsta

Lock Down Publications
P.O. Box 870494
Mesquite, Tx 75180

Visit our website at www.lockdownpublications.com

Cover design and layout by: **Dynasty's Cover Me**
Book interior design by: **Shawn Walker**
Edited by: **Jill Duska**

Stay Connected with Us!

Text **LOCKDOWN** to 22828 to stay up-to-date with new releases, sneak peaks, contests and more…

Submission Guideline

Submit the first three chapters of your completed manuscript to ldpsubmissions@gmail.com, subject line: Your book's title. The manuscript must be in a .doc file and sent as an attachment. Document should be in Times New Roman, double spaced and in size 12 font. Also, provide your synopsis and full contact information. If sending multiple submissions, they must each be in a separate email.

Have a story but no way to send it electronically? You can still submit to LDP/Ca$h Presents. Send in the first three chapters, written or typed, of your completed manuscript to:

LDP: Submissions Dept
Po Box 870494
Mesquite, Tx 75187

*DO NOT send original manuscript. Must be a duplicate. *

Provide your synopsis and a cover letter containing your full contact information.

Thanks for considering LDP and Ca$h Presents.

Nicholas Lock

Prologue

Taz had just dropped his daughters off at Tyshae's house when Isabella's cherry-red Mercedes cut him off. She stuck her head out the window and yelled "Pull the fuck over!"

He thought about ignoring her, but he didn't know what lengths she was going to go to in order to get his attention. Taz still hadn't talked to her since the meeting with her father. He pulled over at a Kangaroo gas station and got out as Isabella swerved in behind him. The car had barely come to a stop and she was already out of the car and charging in his direction. She wasted no time. When she got in reach, she started raining down blows on him.

"Why the fuck you ain't been home? Why you didn't answer your phone?" She continued to punch on him.

"Stop fucking hitting me!" Taz yelled, grabbing her arms. "You ain't got the right to question me! You don't fucking listen. I told your ass to stay the hell home and what did you do?" He shook her.

"Take your hands off her," some white dude said.

"Mind your fucking business!" Taz said.

Before Taz could react, the man hit him in the side of the head, causing him to let Isabella go and stumble against his car.

"He told you to mind your business, so that's what the hell you need to do." Isabella thrust her ever-present .380 in his face.

He threw his hands up and backed away "You got it, Miss."

"Put that gun up, Bella," Taz told her as the dude got in his car and sped away.

"I should shoot you," she admitted, tucking her gun away.

"Now take your ass home, Bella."

"Not unless you bring your ass with me."

"That's the shit I be talking about right there! You don't listen to shit I say! And you wonder why I ain't been home?" Taz blanked, rubbing his hand down his face.

"You know what? Fuck you!" She stormed off towards her car.

As Taz turned to get in his car, she called his name. He started not to turn around, but something in her voice caught his attention. His face fell when he turned around. There stood Gutta and four other dread heads, and Gutta had a gun pointed at Isabella's head. Taz knew he didn't have a shot in hell of reaching her before Gutta did.

"Zion said laugh now, cry lata, and it's lata." Gutta shot Isabella in the face.

"Nooo!" Taz yelled.

Chapter 1

It was the first Sunday of the month and Club Diamond was lit! Anybody who was somebody was out tonight. There were plenty of hoes out. Of course, the jackboys were there in full force, eyeing the D-boys as a lion eyes her prey. In the midst of the crowd stood Taz, TK, PJ, and Reggie, who didn't really fit into any group in particular. For instance, PJ didn't know what he wanted to do. Sometimes he sold a little 'caine, but it never lasted long. TK sold crack, but he had been copping the same two ounces since '06 and here it was 2017. Reggie played with the loud – played, because he always found a way to fall off. Taz, on the other hand, didn't sell anything. He was fresh home from an eight year bid for murder and a robbery charge. He originally had 13 to 16 years, but a time cut got him home early. He was a 9-to-5 nigga at the moment, working at Smithfield Packaging. Before he went in, though, he was a full-blown jackboy with no regards for human life. Now he just wanted to remain free and take care of his two daughters.

"Damn, nigga, why you so quiet?" TK asked Taz, who was standing on the wall taking it all in.

"Chilling, my nigga. You know I ain't been out like this in a long time."

"You know this the nigga first club scene since coming home, so he don't know what to do with himself. We had to damn near beg the nigga to come out tonight," PJ said.

"All he want to do is go to work and go home."

"Let me find out prison done really squared you up," TK joked.

"Fuck you, nigga." Taz laughed "I just ain't trying to get back in the mix. This the same thing that was going on before I left. The same niggas out here stunting with they re-up money, same hoes out here wearing outfits with the tag still on so they can return it tomorrow. Then you got these counterfeit jackboys that all they want to do is take a nigga chain and a couple bands and think they did something. These scenes just put me in a mindset that I really don't want to go back to," he said seriously.

And they all knew what mindset that was. Out of the four, Taz was the livewire. PJ got wild too, but Taz put the fear of God in niggas when he got on his bullshit. Before he went in, he had a penchant for violence and mayhem, but prison had calmed him down and turned him into a thinker. There was still some of the old Taz around, but it took a lot to bring it out. You'd never be able to tell because he almost always had a smile on his face.

"Y'all stall my nigga out. Besides, y'all know y'all don't want him back on his bullshit," Reggie said insincerely.

Truth be told, that's exactly what Reggie wanted because he knew if he got Taz back to his old self, the city was going to have a transferring of power. And the four of them would be in the driver seat.

"Y'all ain't talking about shit." Taz laughed, heading towards the bar. "Let me get two shots of Goose," he told the half-naked bartender. After downing both shots, he turned back and surveyed the scene once again. He thought back to the last time he was in the club, which was the same night he caught his charge...

***

It was October 2009 and he was in Club Ciroc stunting like a fool! This night in particular, he was really on his shit. He was sporting some black Levi's, a grey thermal, some black and grey 7's, and an Oakland Raiders fitted. If the rose gold chain with the larger than life Jesus piece didn't catch your eye, then the diamond-studded Presidential Rolex would.

"What's good, playboy?" Big Sean, his baby sister's on again/off again, asked, putting his hand out for some dap.

"Minding my business," Taz replied, ignoring the outstretched hand.

"You still salty about that situation with me and Tyshae?"

"Yo, check this: keep my little sister's name out your mouth. The only reason you still got life in your body is because she begged me not to do anything to you. So nah, I ain't salty at all," Taz said, smiling. "But next time you decide to put your hands on something I love, make sure your mama got your life insurance paid up," he said, heading back towards the V.I.P. section.

"Where you been, boo?" Keishana asked, climbing all over him.

"We thought you had forgot about us." Mary pouted.

"Y'all should've known better than that. Besides, I got big plans for us tonight," he said, palming both their asses.

"Can you handle that, daddy?" Mary asked, licking his ear.

"Only time will tell," Taz said, sitting down on the leather couch.

"So we going home with you?" asked Keishana.

Laughing, Taz said, "You know that's dead. Candace'll put y'all in the dirt."

"Anyway," Mary said, rolling her neck.

"We going to the Hilton. Now sit back and relax. Better yet, roll this up." he passed her some O.G. Kush.

As they sat in V.I.P. burning, Taz scanned the crowd for the real reason he was in the club. After about five minutes, he spotted Quadree at the bar whispering in a pretty dark-skinned chick's ear. With all the jewelry he had on, Taz didn't realize

11

how he had missed him in the first place. He had to have on at least a quarter mil worth of jewels on. Little did Quadree know, tonight was probably going to be his last on earth. Quadree - or Quad, as everyone called him - had Fayetteville on lock as far as the coke game went. But that was getting ready to come to an end, because he was in the crosshairs of one of the city's deadliest jackboys. Quad came from Miami with the best work Fayetteville - or better yet, North Carolina - had seen in a long time. From the outside looking in, you'd mistake him for an average hood nigga, but he was anything but. At 5'6" and 115 pounds, he was little in stature, but he more than made up for it with his aggressive demeanor. To top it off, he had an army of Haitians that he brought with him from Miami, plus he was said to have ties with Zoe Pound Mafia.

None of that was going to deter Taz tonight though. He had been following Quad for the last three weeks, so he had his routine down to a T. He knew Quad was a full-blown trick, and every time he went to a club or party, he took a girl with him - not to a hotel, but to the place he laid his head at every night.

"What's on your mind, daddy?" Mary asked, running her hands over the waves in his head.

"Me in you," he said, standing up. "Let's go."

Mary and Keishana hurried up and grabbed their tote bags. They made sure to lock eyes with every woman in the club as they followed Taz out in an attempt to rub it in that they got chosen by one of the city's more notorious go-getters.

"I got the front!" Keishana yelled, running towards his candy-red Denali.

"Ugh," Mary said, frustrated. "You make me sick."

"You good, ma," he said, laughing. "That just means you get to ride this dick first," Taz told her, slapping her on the butt.

"You know what your responsibility is, Ms. I-got-the-front?" he asked, climbing in the truck.

"What?" Keishana asked, clueless.

"This." He pulled his dick out. "Go ahead and show me what that mouth like."

The whole ride to the Hilton, all you heard was Keishana slurping and sucking on his dick. Just as they pulled into the hotel parking lot, Taz blessed her with a throat full of kids. "Uh uh," he said, pushing her head back down as she tried to come up, "swallow all that."

"I'm on some otha shit, I'm dressed in all black, I'm wit' my niggas, damn, and all of us strapped, we on some killa shit, somebody getting whacked, you know I mean business when I'm in all black." Plies's "All Black" ringtone came through on Taz's phone.

After reading the text message, Taz said, "Here go the room key. It's Room 327. I got to go make a play real quick."

"Okay. And you better not take all day," Mary, the more aggressive of the two, responded.

"Just keep that pussy wet until I come back."

As soon as he pulled off, he went into killer mode. He knew he had to be on his shit or he would be the one in front of a barrel. With all the money Quadree was getting, he was still staying in the middle class neighborhood. The houses were mostly two stories, but they weren't luxurious.

After pulling into the neighborhood, Taz cut his headlights off and cruised down the street. He parked his truck on the next street over, put a hoody on, and pulled his ski mask down over his face. Feelings of nervousness washed over him as he crept up to the back of the house. He always had the jitters before a lick, but this time was a little different. Ignoring it, he checked to make sure he had one in the head of his Glock 19 and eased the back door open. Listening, he heard Quadree talking somewhere upstairs. He crept through the first floor, making sure there weren't any unexpected surprises. Satisfied, he made his way up the stairs towards the voices.

"G'on, put it in ya mouth, gal," Quadree said.

When Taz peeked in the room, he saw that Quad was sitting on the edge of the bed naked with the dark-skinned chick from the club on her knees with his dick in her hand.

"Mi don't got all night," he said, grabbing the back of her head.

"Put this in your mouth, nigga!" Taz rushed the room, forcing the Glock in his mouth, knocking one of his front teeth loose.

"Nigga! What took you so fucking long?" she amped. "I almost had to put that shit in my mouth!"

"Keasha, shut up!"

Taz and Keasha - or Kiki, for short - were best friends. Whenever it came time to put in some work or set a nigga up, she was down, especially since she felt like she owed Taz her life. They met under similar circumstances. Taz was in Atlanta two years ago pulling a lick. When he ran in the spot, the nigga he was there to rob had a young girl between his legs jacking him off. Come to find out the girl was his niece and she was only sixteen. In the end, he killed the nigga and Keasha ended up coming back to Fayetteville with him. Since then, they had formed a brother/sister bond that was unbreakable.

"Check this, homeboy. Go ahead and tell me where everything at and we can be on our way."

"Fuck you, bombaclot! Ya know who mi is?"

***

"You okay, boo?" the bartender asked, snapping him out

of his reverie.

"Yeah, shawty, I'm good," he responded, heading back towards his boys.

When he walked up, his boys were in the process of putting their game down on a group of women. Not to be left out, he noticed a pretty redbone in a yellow suit not talking to anyone, so he tried his hand.

"Say, ma, why you over here by yourself?"

"Anyway," she said after looking him up and down.

"Damn, it's like that?"

"Yeah, it's like that!" she yelled. "You can't do nothing with a bitch like me. I mean, look at you and look at me. Really. You in here looking like Farmer John with that plain Jane-ass outfit. Nigga, please!" she said looking over at her girls.

"Girl, you wrong for that," the chick PJ was talking to said.

"Ha, nah, she good. I ain't tripping," Taz said, rocking a smile

"Nah, nigga, you is tripping since you came out here looking like a clown," she continued.

"Ha, ha, ha, bitch, do you know who the fuck you talking to? Don't get that shit confused. I'm not one of these suckers you used to dealing with. My name's Taz, bitch! You better recognize a boss when you see one. You better put some respect on that shit before you make the front page."

Seeing the surprised look on her face, Taz knew he got his point across, especially the way her homegirl's eyes got big when he said his name. Being gone eight years hadn't lessened the weight his name held in the city.

"I'ma catch up with y'all niggas later," he said, walking out of the club.

Reggie sat watching Taz leave with a smile on his face because he knew it was only a matter of time before Taz got back to the streets - or so he hoped.

Chapter 2

"Um, Daddy, can we get an iPad? Taz's youngest daughter Nevaeh asked

"Do y'all deserve it?"

"Yes!" D'Azia yelled, climbing into his lap.

"Just the other day you was too big for my kisses, now y'all all in my lap."

"Only in public, Dad."

It was the day after the club, and Taz was spending some quality time with his daughters. They were both his twins. You would've thought he spit them out himself, especially Neveah, because she had his dark brown-skinned complexion and his attitude while D'Azia was a lighter brown and was real shy. They were his whole reason for living. The whole time he was locked up, they were all he thought about - them and his sister. He had to watch them grow up through pictures and visits. When they gave him his time cut, he promised himself he wasn't going to miss another day of their lives. When he left, Neveah and D'Azia were one and two, now they were nine and ten.

"So, what we doing today?" he asked.

"The movies!" D'Azia hollered.

"Skating rink," Neveah countered.

"How about we do both? Now go get dressed."

"We ain't forgot about the iPad either," Neveah said before taking off to her room.

Taz just smiled and shook his head, thinking how much of a problem she was going to be as she got older.

"Neveah, what do you got on? You not going nowhere with me with that outfit on." He laughed at her mismatched outfit. She had on some lime green tights, a hot pink shirt, and some orange and black Air Max's. "You know what? I don't care. Let's go."

The whole ride to the skating rink he was peppered with questions about whether or not he was going to get some iPads.

"Daddy, do you love my mama?" D'Azia asked out of nowhere.

"Why you ask me that?"

"Just want to know."

"Yeah, I love both y'all mamas, but we just not boyfriend and girlfriend."

What he really wanted to say was that their mamas weren't shit! They both had turned their backs on him when he got his time - more so D'Azia's mom Alicia. She got married and at one point in time, she tried to give D'Azia her husband's last name. As for Neveah's mother Tamika, she made Taz's mother her legal guardian so he wasn't as hot with her, but she still wasn't shit in his eyes.

Once they got to the skating rink, his girls were in full go mode. After they got their skates, that was all she wrote. All they wanted to do was be on the skate floor. As he watched them have a good time, someone tapped him on the shoulder.

"Um, I'm not trying to bother you or nothing, but you look mad familiar. What's your name?" a brown-skinned chick with a pixie cut asked.

As Taz got to looking her over, he was thinking the same thing, that she looked familiar as hell. Then it dawned on him. The pixie cut threw him off, but the body was still the same, if not better.

"Mary?" he said, calling her name.

"Where you know me from?" she asked, rolling her neck in classic ghetto Mary style.

"I see you ain't changed a bit, still ghetto fabulous. But yo, you don't recognize the nigga that was gon' blow your back out?" he asked, leaning back against the wall.

"What? Nigga, you don't - " She stopped mid-sentence and really looked at Taz and her eyes got big. "Oh my God! Taz!" she squealed, jumping on him.

"Don't act like you missed me. You ain't send me not one letter the whole time I was locked up," he said, pushing her away.

"I was mad at you! You left us in that room, talking about you was coming back. The next thing I know, my phone start blowing up and the whole city talking about how you had killed ole boy Quadree. If you would've stayed with me and Keishana, you would've never got jammed up," she said, putting her hand on her hips.

Nodding his head, he once again got to thinking about how things went wrong that night...

***

"Yeah, I know who you is, but if you knew who I was, you would've been told me what I wanted to know."

"Man, watch out."

Boom! Boom! Keasha shot Quadree in the chest. "You was wasting your time and mine," she quickly said upon seeing the look on Taz's face. "I know where everything at."

"Well, come on then."

"Everything in the garage," she said, leading the way.

As they were making their way through the house, he saw a shadow shoot past the window and he stopped. When Keasha looked back and saw Taz standing there, she said, "Nigga, come on!"

He put a finger to his lips, silencing her, and motioned to the front of the house. As he started to creep towards the living room, the front door got kicked in and a swarm of black-clad figures rushed in with ski masks on.

Before he raised his gun, they screamed, "FBI! Lower your weapon!"

Next thing he knew, he got slammed on the ground and thrown in handcuffs. When he looked to where Keasha was standing, he saw her disappear in the garage.

***

"Taz! Taz! Taz!" Mary yelled, bringing him back to the present.

"What, girl?"

"Did you hear me?"

"Nah, what you say?"

"What is you doing at the skating rink?"

"Daddy, Daddy did you see us?" his daughters asked, skating up to him before he could answer.

"Yeah, I seen y'all big heads out there falling everywhere. Y'all ready to eat something yet?"

"Oh, you not going to introduce us?" Mary asked.

Little did she know, Taz really had no intention of doing any introductions. He tried to keep his family life and the streets separate.

"D'Azia, Neveah, this is Mary. Mary, these my daughters."

"Oh my God, y'all are so pretty. I want y'all to meet my son," she said, looking around. "I be right back."

"Come on, let's get some fries and nachos," Taz said, leading the way.

"Who was that lady?" D'Azia asked.

"Just somebody I knew a while ago, nosy."

After they got their food and drinks and were making their way to a booth to sit down. Mary walked up with a little boy in tow.

"Y'all, this is my son Keishawn," she said, sitting down beside Taz.

After the introductions were made, her son took back off to the game section and D'Azia and Neveah went back on the skate floor without taking one bite to eat, leaving Taz alone with a talkative Mary.

"I didn't know you had no kids," she said, shocked.

"You wasn't supposed to know, and when I left, I know for a fact you ain't have none."

"I know, I had him six years ago. Really, he was the best thing that could've happened to me. He forced me to get my shit together. For real, nigga!" she said upon seeing the smirk on Taz's face. "I went back to school, got my nursing license and everything," she stated proudly.

"So you don't hang with Keishana no more?"

"Of course I do! That's my road dog, But I just don't give it up like I used to," she said sincerely, making him think she really had changed.

"What about Keishana? Matter of fact, what's her number?" he asked, remembering the good head she gave.

"I'll give it to you, but you got to promise me you not gon' fuck her."

"Ohhh, you hating," he laughed. "Damn, what's up?" he asked upon seeing the sad look on her face.

"Look, don't tell her I told you this because she don't be telling people. I know she fucked with you like, that but she got AIDS."

"Stop lying on that woman."

"That's on my son. I'm the only one that knows. She still looks the same, but my girl dying slow."

"Damn, who gave it to her?"

"She won't tell me. She said she gon' handle it herself."

"That's wild."

"In other news, what made you grow dreads? I always took you for a clean cut nigga," she said, grabbing some nachos off his plate.

"Most of the barbers in prison can't cut, plus I just wanted to switch it up. What, you don't like them?"

"Yeeaah!"

"So does that mean me and you gon' finish where we left off eight years ago?"

"Maybe, maybe not. But here go Keishana's number, I know she wanna talk to you, and here's mine too. I got to go, but call whenever." She got up, kissed him on the cheek, and then sashayed away, throwing her hips way harder than was necessary.

"I got to have some of that...after she take an AIDS test," he said to himself, then set out in search of his babies.

Chapter 3

Taz had just gotten off work and his phone wouldn't stop ringing. He'd had a long day and really wasn't in the mood to be bothered. He looked at his phone again and didn't recognize the number, so he let it go to the voicemail. Then the same number called right back.

"Who this?" Taz asked aggressively

"Why did I have to hear from the streets that you was home? Huh, nigga?" a female asked angrily.

The voice was mad and familiar, but he couldn't place it right off the bat.

"Who is this?"

"Oh, word? So you don't know a bitch voice no more, D'angelo?"

Instantly he knew who it was, and a smile crept to his face. Only a select few individuals called him by his government name. Just hearing her voice brought on a wave of emotions - some of them not so good, but for the most part it was love.

"Kiki, you got a lot of explaining to do," he said, trying to keep the happiness out of his voice.

"I know, nigga, and I got a surprise for you," she said excitedly.

"I don't do surprises, Kiki, and where you at?"

"I'll be back in Fayetteville in the morning. I had to make a move real quick."

"Yeah, and like I said, you got a lot of explaining to do."

"Bye, Father, love you."

"Whatever. Love you too."

Taz rode the rest of the way home in silence, processing the conversation he'd just had with his partner in crime. He knew a lot of things could change in an eight year period, and he was hoping Keasha wasn't one of them.

"Yo, I ain't know you was still on talking terms with Kiki," TK said, passing PJ a blunt after hearing Taz tell them he was meeting Kiki tomorrow.

Taz, PJ, TK, and Reggie were all at TK's spot in Cambridge Arms chilling, Taz was sipping on an Icehouse while the rest of them passed blunts of Kush around.

"Why you say that?" Taz asked curiously.

"You know when you had first got jammed up, niggas was saying she had set you up, this, that, and the third? Because everybody knew that was your other half when it came to hitting a lick. Then when you was the only one that got locked up, it just looked funny."

"Yo, check game," Taz said, getting ready to tell a story that only two people knew. "First off, she good money. Second, that nigga Quadree was working with the Feds. When everything went down, the FBI rushed the spot, not the city police. I found all this out when I got my motion discovery. I really wasn't supposed to get that much time because they couldn't prove shit!"

"Bro, you was in the house with a dead body," PJ said with a "duh nigga" look on his face.

Taz just smiled before saying "Yeah, but the gun I got caught with wasn't the murder weapon, plus they did the gunshot residue test on the scene and it was negative. And for all they know, he could've invited me in. Not to mention the fact that they never found the murder weapon."

"So why in the hell did you take that plea?" Reggie asked, confused.

"Honestly, the way I look at it, I was doing time for all the shit I hadn't got caught for. And how many times you gon' see on the news where a man gets set free after twenty-five years of prison time and it just comes out he was wrongly convicted? It was a chance I wasn't willing to take."

"Hold up. If that wasn't the gun that killed him and you never fired a gun that night, that means somebody else did," PJ said.

"No shit, Sherlock," Reggie joked.

"And we should all know who that somebody was," TK stated the obvious.

"Boy, when you got locked up, she went on a rampage. Couldn't nobody tell her shit. She was burning them Zoe Pound niggas left and right, and they was running down on niggas something serious. What made it so bad was all the other so-called goons and thugs was running to us trying to get us to holler at her, but that was a lost cause. That's when I came to see you. Whatever you said to her calmed her all the way down," TK said.

"So what, y'all about to terrorize the city again, or is you still on your 9-to-5 shit?" Reggie wanted to know.

"Nah, I'm cooling, I ain't messing around."

As badly as he wanted to, he just couldn't bring himself to hop back in the streets, but seeing and being back around his niggas, the pull was there, especially seeing how fresh his boys were. A lot had changed since he had been gone. They had all grown into men. When Taz left, he was the tallest of the four, but now he and Reggie both stood 6'2". Taz was twenty-eight while Reggie was twenty-six. Reggie was just a little heavier between the two. And he was the self-proclaimed swag king. PJ and TK were both thirty and both stood 5'9", but other than that and their dreads, they were opposites. While PJ wanted to get lit, TK would rather chill. PJ was flamboyant and TK played the background. Through it all, though, they were all thick as thieves, and that included Keasha. They all looked at her like one of the crew. With all the different personalities, Taz was the glue that kept it all together.

"Oh yeah, boy! The city buzzing like a fool about you now! Them hoes from the club ran they mouth about you and my phone been jumping ever since. It's mostly these scary-ass niggas just trying to see what kind of time you on. They shook," PJ stated.

"They ain't got nothing to worry about as long as they stay in they lane," Taz said.

"Guess who I ran into?" TK asked.

"Who?"

"Yo' wifey, Candace."

"Fuck that bitch with an AIDS dick, my nigga!"

"Damn, what she do to make you feel like that?" Reggie asked.

"I thought I told y'all, but it must've been Kiki I told. That bitch ran off with all my bread I had put up and disappeared on a nigga," he said, getting mad just thinking about it.

"Why you ain't say nothing? You know we would've handled that," TK said

"Nah, Kiki wanted to too, but I told her no. I still got a soft spot for her, so I just let her live," he said, looking off.

They all knew that other than his kids and his sister, his world revolved around Candace. He had turned her from a busted hoodrat to a high-class woman. Whatever she asked for, she got, no questions asked. She had designer everything. Even her lingerie was designer. She was the real diamond princess. And for her to do that to him had hurt him in the worst way.

"Ooohh shit!" PJ said, hopping up, walking back and forth with the blunt in his hand.

"What the hell wrong with you? And pass the damn blunt," Reggie said.

"It all makes sense now. Remember how all of a sudden that nigga SK got on? I was wondering how he just popped up selling weight," PJ said.

"PJ, I'm trying to figure out what that got to do with what we was talking about," Taz said.

No one said anything. They were all just looking at Taz.

"What the fuck y'all looking at, and why you ain't answered my question, nigga?"

"Bro, that's who Candace started messing with after you got locked up."

"Word. And you say the nigga chewing, huh?" The wheels were turning in his head.

"Yeah, I mean, he a young nigga. I used to front packs to him, then one day he tell me he got Zanes for sale," PJ said.

"I ain't tripping. I'm happy she got a sponsor. But it better not come out that she was his sponsor."

With that said, Taz left, leaving them to wonder what he was going to do if he found out that Candace had used his money to help SK get on.

The next morning, Taz was standing on his porch with butterflies in his stomach, waiting for Kiki to pull up. Allot of people thought they were fucking back in the day because of how close they were. Candace accused them of fucking plenty of times. It was nothing to see Kiki curled up in Taz's lap. But they had never crossed that line. They really were best friends. She knew his secrets and he knew hers. They were so much alike it was like they were twins. That's the type of bond they had. He heard her way before he saw her.

"You couldn't fuck with me if you wanted to," Cardi B rapped out of the speakers.

Kiki bent the corner in a smoke-grey Cadillac Escalade. As soon as the truck stopped, she ran and hopped in his arms.

"Oh, you missed me, trick?" Taz joked.

"Did I? More that you know. I been out here going crazy without your crazy ass."

"Get off me let me check you out."

The last time Taz had seen Kiki was on the visitation screen eight years ago. He had her promise not to come back because he felt like the police knew he wasn't by himself and he didn't want her to catch a case.

"Damn! Where you get all this ass from?" he asked, slapping her on the butt playfully.

"Atlanta. I went and got some ass shots. You know I already had plenty of titties," she said grabbing her double D's.

"You still 'bout retarded." Taz laughed.

Before he left, Kiki was a real slim chick with a big chest and a little butt, but now she had blossomed into a full-blown woman. She was always pretty, but now she was drop dead gorgeous. Her pitch black skin was flawless. She was a stallion at 5'7" and 145 pounds, all curves. Her features were majestic. She had beautiful long legs, a small waist, a super fat ass, and full breasts, loading up to a round face with gray, doe-shaped eyes. She could go for an African queen.

"Come on." Taz led her in the house.

"Nigga, you done got big! And your hair about as long as mine," she said, grabbing his dreads that hung just below his chest.

"That ain't yours, Kiki," he said, referring to her silky black hair that fell to the top of her ass.

"Not true. I just never let it grow before," she admitted.

"Fuck all that, explain to me how you didn't get caught in that house that night." Taz raised his brow.

"Honestly, if they really would've searched, they probably would've found me. When they came in the garage, I was hiding under this big-ass grill he had," she responded, taking a seat on his wrap around sofa. "They stayed in the garage searching maybe five minutes, but I still didn't come out until the whole house got quiet a good four hours later. I got the work and bread and took off."

"So you did get the stuff?" he asked, surprised.

"That was my surprise to you. I got it all in the truck. Altogether it was ten bricks and two hundred bands," she responded, heading back out the door to go grab the work and money.

Damn, Taz thought to himself. This is just what he needed, since after Candace took all his money, he was left with nothing. And working his 9-to-5 was barely covering all his expenses, even with overtime. Then his daughters wanted everything in the store and he refused to let them go without. But he still wasn't going back to the streets. After he sold his half of the work, he'd be straight for a little minute, he thought to himself.

"So you not gon' help me?" Kiki was in the doorway, out of breath.

"You made it this far. I figured you was good." He smiled before grabbing a bag.

"Look, Taz, I know that bum bitch took you down, so all this yours. I'm good. I been doing my little one two. But now that you home, I know it's about to go all the way down.

"Nah, Kiki, I'm done with all that."

She just stared at him like he was growing wings. She put her hand to his forehead.

"Are you sick? Do you need me to take you to the ER?"

"Move, girl," he chuckled. "Nah, I'm just chilling, Kiki. I just did eight years in a box and I really ain't trying to go back."

"You not! We move too cautious for that. The only reason you went away that time was because Quadree was a rat," she tried to reason with him.

He just shook his head. "It's over, Kiki, my heart just not

in it. We can go legit and start our own business or something," he tried reasoning with her.

"Legit! Legit don't make this in a few hours of work!" she yelled, kicking one of the bags, causing money to fly everywhere. "This is all I know, it's all you ever taught me." The tears were beginning to fall.

Before he could respond, she walked out the door, leaving him with a floor full of money and a heavy heart.

Chapter 4

Since Taz had been home, it had been all work, no play, but tonight it was playtime. For the last few days, he and Mary had been talking on the phone, getting to know each other. From what he could tell, she had really turned over a new leaf. He just hoped she didn't have her mind set on anything serious, because he just couldn't look past how loose she was back in the day. Once a hoe, always a hoe.

Tonight he was stepping out on his fly shit. He had on some Akoo blue jeans, an orange and while Akoo button-up, and some orange and white Space Jams. His dreads were cornrowed to the back in two braids. He would've paid to have his presidential Rolex right now, but Candace took all his jewelry too. He did still have his Frank Muller watch, so he was still to the good. After wholesaling the binds, he had updated his wardrobe, and his dress game was back to where it was before he left. He just had to get his jewels back up. And he had traded his Camry in for the new Cadillac CT6.

After putting on a few dabs of Jean Paul Gaultier, he was out the door. Riding through the city on the way to Mary's house, he got lost in his thoughts. Before he had left, in so many ways he was the man in the city. He missed the glitz and glamour that came with the lifestyle. But every time he got the thought of hopping back in the game, he thought back to that cell and watching his girls grow up through pictures.

His crew didn't know what it was like to have their freedom taken away, to eat when someone told you to eat, sleep when they told you. He'd rather die than go through that again. It had been a few days and he hadn't heard from Kiki since that day she dropped the bread off. He was going to have to make things right sooner or later.

He called Mary and said, "I'm outside" as he pulled up to

her apartment.

"Damn" he stated as she came out of her apartment in a form-fitting yellow Fendi dress. "You did that," Taz told her as she sat down.

"You looking handsome yourself."

"Don't I always? Look, though." He turned to face her. "I know we was supposed to go out to eat, but seeing you in that dress, there's been a slight change in plans."

"What?" she asked, disappointed.

"Me with your feet on my shoulders as I taste that pussy." Taz licked his lips.

"Boy, stop playing." She blushed.

"I'm dead serious. If you really want to go out, we can, but if not, we going to the room. So what's up?"

"The room," she responded bashfully.

Hearing her response, Taz headed in the direction of the nearest hotel, which just so happened to be the same Hilton which they were at eight years ago.

"Why you so quiet? I know you not scared," Taz said, pulling into the parking lot.

"Anyways." She rolled her eyes, getting out of the car.

He paid for the room and as soon as they hit the door, he was all over her.

"Let me go freshen up first." She stepped out of his grasp.

"Go ahead and handle your business."

As Mary went to the bathroom, Taz took in the décor of the room. The white and beige set off the perfect, relaxed kind of atmosphere. Pulling back the curtains revealed a huge window overlooking downtown. Going to the bar, he poured a shot of Patron. Mary came back out just as he was downing his drink.

"That dress gon' look real good on the floor," he said, taking her into his arms.

"So what's the hold up?" she asked seductively.

He turned her around and unzipped the back, causing it to fall to the floor. When she turned back around to face him, his mouth watered at the sight of her hardened nipples. He heard her gasp as he took one of her nipples in his mouth. He picked her up and carried her to the king-sized bed, never taking his mouth off Mary's breasts. She sat up and watched as he removed his shirt, then his pants. Her breath got caught in her throat when she saw his dick straining against the material of his Polo boxers.

"It's too late for that." He smirked

"Hold up." She stopped him as he tried to crawl between her legs. "Let me blow this."

She pulled his boxers down and grabbed his semi-hard dick. Once she ran her tongue around the rim, he stretched all the way out. She held eye contact as she ran her tongue the length of his dick. Taz grabbed the back of her head and slid all the way to the back of her throat.

"Damn, ma," he mumbled, getting lost in her oral talents.

Mary squeezed the base tightly, all the while bringing him in and out of her mouth.

"Sssss…" he hissed, gripping her hair.

Taking him out of her mouth, she stroked him a few times, then went back to trying to swallow him whole. Gripping his ass, she pulled him all the way into her mouth and down her throat. Taz started to fuck her mouth as if he was in some pussy.

"I'm about to nut up."

Mary used the suction of her jaws to help him to his release. She let most of it into her mouth and the rest run down his dick.

"You a nasty bitch." Taz commented.

"Only for you."

"Scoot up," he commanded while grabbing a Magnum and sliding it on. He took her in, laying open and waiting for him. He climbed her legs and placed the tip at her opening.

"Be easy with me. It's been awhile," she warned.

"Oh shit" were the words that left his lips as he entered her inch by inch. Her pussy was virgin tight. It was going to take everything he had not to bust early. Mary smirked as if reading his mind.

"Oh yeah," he said. "I got something for you." He pushed her legs back, damn near making her knees touch her ears.

"Nooo, Taz." Her eyes got big, knowing he was about to put some work in.

He slid all the way in, causing her to holler out. With every stroke, he hit the bottom, causing her pussy to get wetter and wetter.

"Taaaz," she whined, putting her hand on his stomach, trying to control how deep he went.

He grabbed her wrist and pinned it to the bed. He started moving in sync to her moans as he tried to knock her walls down.

"I'm about to cum," she whispered, causing him to go into overdrive. As her pussy started to squeeze his dick, he knew she was on the brink.

"Flip over so I can get these back shots."

Mary lazily got on her hands and knees, putting an arch in her back, causing her pussy to poke out. As soon as Taz entered her, she started throwing her ass back and squeezing at the same time, causing her cat to grip his pole. Taz felt himself about to bust. He tried to slow down his strokes, but she was having none of it. She started rocking back into him.

"Do your thang then, baby girl," he said, watching his dick slide in and out of her hot spot.

Mary screamed out in pleasure as another orgasm rocked through her body. A few strokes later, Taz released inside the condom and lay down on his back, reveling in the aftermath of their fuck session.

Mary took off his condom and cleaned him off with her mouth, at the same time causing him to harden back up. The last thing he remembered was Mary swallowing a mouthful of kids as he dozed off.

Nicholas Lock

Chapter 5

Since coming home, Taz had yet to talk to his little sister. They had fallen out while he was locked up because she kept going back to her boyfriend, even though he had the habit of putting his hands on her. He was on his way to her house so they could catch up, plus he wanted to take her shopping. The eight years he was gone forced her to get her shit together instead of depending on him. She had worked her way up to manager at Wells Fargo and she was now making six figures a year.

"What's up, little sis?" he asked as she got in the car.

"Little sis? You ain't nothing but four months older than me." She rolled her eyes.

"I'm still older."

Taz and Tyshae had the same pops, but different mothers. They had the bond of kids that grew up in the same house. The whole ride to the mall, they informed each other of what had been going on in their personal lives. As soon as Tyshae's feet hit the pavement, she was dashing into the mall on full go mode. She knew Taz wasn't going to hold anything back when it came to her and she planned on taking full advantage of it. She had plans on going into every shoe and clothing store available. She hadn't been able to do that since he'd been gone. Just seeing his sister with a smile on her face made Taz's day.

They had been in the mall going on two hours when a female called his name.

"D'angelo?"

When he turned around to see who it was, he didn't recognize the redbone in front of him. She was all the way like that. She was designer down even her earrings were Chanel. He was getting ready to put his G down until she removed her Chanel glasses. His mood immediately turned sour. He turned to walk away and she grabbed his arm to stop him.

"Candace, you better get your hands off me," he warned, turning back to face her.

"So that's how you gon' treat me?" she asked, poking her lips out and putting on her sad face, the one Taz was always a sucker for. Feeling the barriers he had built up beginning to crumble, he turned to leave again and she grabbed his arm a second time. When he turned back around, he saw all the things that made her so attractive to him: her redbone complexion, her long hair, her perfectly put together features from her naturally-arched eyebrows to her slanted eyes, button nose, and sensual lips. And she had gained weight in all the right places.

"You like what you see?" she asked, turning to the side so he could see her fattened ass.

"What you want?"

"How you been? I know you probably mad, but you never gave me a chance to explain."

"Nothing to explain. You took my shit! The shit I put in work for, shit that you really had no entitlement to," he vented. "I gave your bird ass whatever the fuck you wanted, and instead of being loyal, you gave me your ass to kiss! Fuck you!"

"But that's not the case!" she cried.

"Bitch, you got a lot of nerve to even be showing your face right now," Tyshae said, walking up. "Matter of fact, I should've been beat your ass." Tyshae started putting her hair in a ponytail.

"I'd sit down somewhere, little girl." A dark-skinned dude approached, putting his arm around Candace. "You good, boo?" he asked Candace.

"Nigga, you got the game twisted! Go ahead and get your issue, fuck nigga!" Taz bassed.

"Nah, fuck you!" The dude got hype.

"Come on, SK," Candace pleaded, trying to pull him away.

"You good, bro?" a group of dudes asked SK.

"Y'all niggas better stay in y'all lane!" Taz went in full blown gorilla mode.

"I got two bands for each of y'all to bust that nigga's ass," SK stated

"No!" Candace tried to intervene.

Click Clack!

"I wouldn't do that if I was y'all, unless you ready to meet y'all maker," Kiki said .45 in hand.

"Let me see that hammer, Kiki." Taz reached his hand out.

"Please, Taz, no," pleaded Candace, seeing the malice in his eyes.

SK's eyes narrowed to slits. "So, I finally meet the notorious Taz. Too bad it was under these kind of circumstances. I probably would've had a spot for you on my team," he said. "But you've fucked that up. You got the upper hand and pulled the trigger. Oh, and I appreciate this." He grabbed Candace's ass and led her away.

"Next time I tell you to give me a hammer, give me the fucking hammer! Be at my house tonight at 7," he said and then walked off, leaving Tyshae and Kiki in different moods.

Tyshae was sad because she didn't want her brother back in the streets while Kiki was happier than a kid in a candy store. She knew the streets were no longer safe because her partner in crime was back. They both knew Taz didn't take threats lightly. There was a real good chance SK was about to have his hands full.

Kiki pulled up to Taz's at exactly 7 o'clock. She got out wearing some black skinny jeans, a black long-sleeved shirt, and some black Air Max 95's. When Taz opened the door, she saw he was dressed similarly in all black. She was about to make a joke until she saw the look on Taz's face. She knew that look all too well. The last time she had seen that look was when he had burst in when her uncle was forcing her to jack him off. Her uncle ended up taking a few bullets to the face and she wouldn't be surprised if someone met that same fate tonight.

"What you know about this nigga SK?" Taz went straight into business mode.

"Not a lot, other than the fact that he supplies a majority of the city. When we knocked Quadree off, it left the city up for grabs. And some kind of way, he got the keys to the city and never looked back. He got a mini army, a bunch of young, don't give a fuck niggas that do whatever he say to do, no questions asked.

"I could give two fucks about his boys. I need to know about him and his operation because I'm about to knock him off that little pedestal he sitting on," he said, pacing back and forth.

"Why?" she asked, stopping him in his tracks.

"What kind of question is that?"

"I don't know, you tell me. Just a week ago you told me you was done, and now all of a sudden you trying to get a nigga. I know you not hurting for no money. So what's up?"

"So you questioning me now?" he asked, eyebrow raised.

"Nah, I'm not questioning you; I'm questioning your motives. My intuition is telling me this has nothing to do with money. It's personal. I seen the look on your face when he said he appreciated this and grabbed Candace. I seen the hurt. If don't nobody know you, bro, I do, so don't play me for no fool."

She had hit the nail right on the head. This was more so about Candace than anything else. It did something to him on the inside to see Candace with another nigga. Truth be told, he really wasn't over her, and seeing her yesterday had solidified that. Leave it to Kiki to bring the truth of the matter out.

"You know what, Kiki? You absolutely right. So instead of doing what I initially had planned, we just gon' hit this nigga's pockets up," Taz confided.

"So you back?"

"Nah, not really, I just want to make a point. We about to play a little chess."

"It ain't like it was when you left, bro. Niggas ain't doing too much standing in the trap, so it ain't gon' be easy to get to this nigga."

"Kiki, everybody can get caught slipping, especially when you got a wifey. So follow the pussy and it'll lead you to the Promised Land."

"And I suppose you gon' follow the pussy, huh?" She smirked.

"Nope. You is," he said before answering his phone. "Yo."

"Dis Taz?" a heavily accented voice asked.

"Yeah, who this?"

"Mi been looking fa ya fa awhile. You's a hard man to get in contact with."

Taz wrinkled his brow up. "Quit playing on my phone, yo."

"Oh, mi not playing. Dis Gutta, and mi tink yo owe mi sum money."

Laughing, Taz said, "I don't know no Gutta and I don't owe nobody shit. So find you somebody else's phone to play on. How did you get this number?"

"Maybe this'll refresh ya memory," he said, ignoring the question. "Ya kilt mi cousin Quadree, so not only do ya owe mi, fam, but ya owe da Zoe Pound Mafia too."

"Fuck you, fuck your fam, and fuck the Zoe Pound

Mafia!" Taz said angrily.

Hearing the Zoe Pound Mafia name, Kiki grabbed her hammer.

"Mi tought you'd say dat. Afta dis, maybe ya change ya mind," he said as shots started to ring out.

Boom! Boom! Boom! Boom!

Taz and Keasha jumped to the floor as bullets slammed into the walls of the house. When the shots stopped, they heard tires screeching. They ran outside as a white truck bent the corner. Neither one said a word. They both knew that all that talk about leaving the streets alone had just gone out the window, especially after going back in the house and seeing all the bullet holes in Taz's daughter's room, knowing what could've been.

Chapter 6

The very next day, Taz called a meeting with his immediate circle, which included Kiki, Reggie, PJ, and TK. They were in the back of his favorite restaurant, a Mexican spot called Micasita's. He called the meeting because he wanted to have a full understanding of where they stood because the severity of the situation had changed, and that meant the rules did too. He was about to make sure that they all knew that there was going to be no more half-stepping. If you were going to hustle, then that's what it was going to be. All the being on one week and falling off the next was out the window. Plus he needed a full rundown on the Zoe Pound nigga Gutta. He was putting SK on the back burner until the Zoe Pound issue was settled. He also needed to know what the streets were looking like because if his feelings proved right, there was about to be a lot of bloodshed, and he wanted to know which side the city was going to choose.

"What took y'all so long?" Taz asked when everybody finally walked in.

"Well hello to you too," Kiki responded.

"It was a big wreck on Racford Road, so they had a whole section blocked off," PJ explained.

"A'ight, well check this. Y'all already know the rundown about how these niggas shot my house up. So as much as I was trying to leave the streets alone, that just wasn't in the cards. But I will say this: this ain't no long term thing. I'm going to deal with this Zoe Pound shit, stack some paper, and fall back," Taz informed them.

"What about SK?" TK wanted to know.

"He gon' get his in due time, but the Zoe Pound is the more pressing matter."

"Okay, but just don't underestimate the nigga," TK said.

"What I really want to know is, what's good with these Zoe Pound niggas? Where they be at, who they fuck with, and what position do this clown Gutta play?"

"You said Gutta?" Reggie asked.

"Yeah."

"I heard of him. They say he somebody in that Zoe Pound shit. He not the top dog, but he right there. Matter of fact, you won't believe who his bitch is," PJ stated.

Taz raised his brow.

"That bitch that tried you in the club that night."

"What bitch?" Kiki asked, looking over at Taz.

"Sit your overprotective ass down," TK said, laughing.

"She was just running her mouth, nothing I couldn't handle," Taz reassured her. "So find out where she stay at and I'm going to lay on her, but also, what the streets looking like? When shit start hitting the fan, what side is niggas gon' be on?"

"We gon' reach out and see, but them Zoe Pound niggas not from here, so I can already pretty much tell you what side they gon' choose," Reggie said.

One of the waitresses came up and asked everybody their order.

"Oh, and your number would be nice," PJ tried his hand, but she just smiled and walked away.

"Ooohh," Reggie said, seeing the rejected look on PJ's face.

Taz couldn't front; the Mexican chick was bad, he thought as she walked away to get their food prepared.

"Besides, these niggas don't want no trouble with your pitbull in a skirt. They know if they go against the grain what she gon' do," TK stated, getting back to the matter at hand.

"Why you so quiet? That ain't like you, what you thinking?" Taz wanted to know Kiki's opinion, especially since she was going toe to toe with the Zoe Pound by herself when he got locked up.

Keasha sipped her drink and sat back, looking everybody in the eyes before saying, "Y'all know how I am and how I give it up. All this politicking ain't my style. Just show me the target and I'm going to make his mama cry. In the meantime and between time, I'm just here," Kiki informed them.

They all looked at Taz to see his reaction, and he just smiled. Kiki had never been one for small talk. She just got right down to business. All in all, though, she had good intentions.

"Did you bring the bag Ms. I'm-just-here?" Taz asked.

"It's in the car."

Earlier that morning, Taz and Keasha had hit a lick for some work and they had decided to give it to TK and them so they could get all the way on their feet.

"A'ight, check. Reggie, when we leave, Kiki gon' shoot you five pounds of gas, TK and PJ, she got eighteen zanes of raw for y'all apiece. No more games. Get this fucking money and stack bread! Because when I say I'm done this time, that's word on my daughters, I'm done! Now that we got all the business out the way, yo, PJ, if you don't bag that bitch, I am."

"Who?" he asked.

"That Mexican chick."

Once she came back with the food, PJ tried again to get her number, but she was having none of it. This time Taz got a real good look at her, and she was nothing short of beautiful. She stood about 5'6" with pretty brown skin, a set of perky titties, and what appeared to be a little tootie booty. Her hair was in a bun, but you could tell by how many times it was wrapped that it came at least to the middle of her back.

"Damn, nigga, let her get her face back." Kiki put him on blast, causing the chick to giggle.

"Hater," he said, watching her walk away, and he could swear she had more sway in her hips than last time.

"And since you all up in my shit. When you gon' get a nigga?"

"I got one," she said matter-of-factly, causing everybody to stop eating and look her way.

Ever since Taz had brought Kiki back from ATL, the whole crew had embraced her. She was like everybody's little sister, and they carried it as such. Anytime a nigga showed interest in her, he usually just let it go, because even if he got the approval of PJ, TK, and Reggie, the odds were slim to none that Taz was going to approve. He always told her to get a good college boyfriend, but it seemed all she attracted was street niggas.

"Damn! Why y'all looking like that? If I didn't know no better, I'd think y'all niggas rather I ate pussy." She smirked.

"You act like you ain't never done it," TK said, causing her to flip him the bird.

"You just mad because all I pull is bad bitches while y'all be pulling scallywags." She smirked.

"Yo, fuck that! Who your boyfriend?" Taz asked, pulling his dreads out of his face.

"Right here." She set her .40 on the table. "And he don't ever go soft."

"You mental health as hell," Reggie said as they all laughed.

"Plus I know if I do bring a nigga around, y'all ain't gon' do nothing but run him off."

"Anyway. Yo, come on so I can grab that work and get to this paper." PJ got up.

"That's a good idea," Reggie said.

"Y'all just gon' leave me, huh?" Taz watched as TK got

up to leave with the others.

"Gotta get this money, bro," Reggie said.

"Be gone then." Taz dapped them up before they left.

"I'm gon' hit you later. I think I might have another lick," Kiki said as she left, kissing him on the cheek.

Taz didn't mind being alone. In prison, you were alone most of the time. It gave you time to get your thoughts in order and reflect. He really didn't want to get back in the streets, but it was obvious the Zoe Pound was cut for blood, and he had his family to think about. He thought about just leaving Fayetteville - or rather, leaving North Carolina altogether - but his pride had nixed that idea. But when it was all said and done, Atlanta might have a new resident. He just had to make sure all issues were dealt with beforehand.

"You need anything else?" the waitress asked.

"Matter of fact, I do. Sit down and talk with me for a minute."

She smiled, showing off a set of perfect pearly whites while shaking her head no.

"What, I'm not your type or something?"

She shrugged her shoulders and slid into the seat across from him, letting him know he had her already.

"So what's your name, pretty lady?"

"Isabella. What's yours?"

"Taz. You look kinda young. How old are you?"

"Twenty-one."

"Oh man, you a baby," he said, and she narrowed her eyes and stood up. Taz grabbed her hand before she could take off. "Damn, I was just playing, ma. Look, put my number in your phone so we can talk and I can figure out when you gon' be off. That way I can take your pretty ass out," he said, holding her hand.

He let her go and she handed him her phone and said "Put

it in and I'll think about it."

But he had other plans. He dialed his number and his phone rang in his pocket, then he hung up. She rolled her eyes as he handed her her phone back and walked away. This time he knew for a fact she was switching harder knowing he was looking. He put a fifty dollar tip on the table and left with thoughts of Isabella on his mind.

***

Later that night, Taz was on the west side in a middle class neighborhood called Foxfire. He pulled up to a two-story brick house, checked his holster, and got out. After he rang the doorbell Keishana opened the door looking like a quarter piece. *Mary had to be lying! Ain't no way this bitch has AIDS.* She was thick as fuck! And her dark skin was blemish free. She put you in the mind of Buffy the Body.

"Oh my God!" She jumped in his arms and he made sure he palmed her ass as he carried her in the house and kicked the door closed. He walked into the living room and sat down on the couch with Keishana in his lap.

"Bitch, you ain't miss me," he said, pushing her off his lap.

"I diiiid," she whined, poking her lips out.

"Show me how much." He pulled his rock hard dick out.

Keishana immediately started jacking him off as she got on the floor between his legs. She continued to jack him off and ran her tongue over his balls.

"Stop playing, girl, and suck this dick." Taz grabbed the back of her head and tried to get Keishana to put him in her mouth.

She moved his hand, kissed the head of his dick, and stood up as tears started to run down her face.

"I can't do you like that," she cried.

"Do me like what?" He wanted to hear her say it.

She sat down on the couch and looked at him with a tear-streaked face.

"I'm sick, Taz," she admitted.

"Sick? You look fine to me." Taz continued playing dumb.

"I got AIDS."

Taz got quiet, losing himself in thought. He had almost put himself on the road to a slow death. On another note, he couldn't do anything but admire Keishana because she was a real bitch. Another broad would've sucked his dick and gave him some pussy with no questions asked, and for that, she would always have his respect, and he was going to see to it that she was to the good. He reached over and wrapped his arms around her as she continued to cry.

"It's gon' be alright, yo, but I want to know who gave it to you."

"It don't even matter," she sniffed. "He a bitch-ass nigga."

"Did he know he had it?"

"Yeah, the fuck-ass nigga knew. When I told him he gave it to me, he just shrugged his shoulders and said I should've made him wear a condom."

"Man, who the fuck is it?" Taz wanted to know bad as hell. "And I'ma make sure he get what he deserves."

"That's really why I been waiting on you to get out, because I know you would take care of it for me. Plus he be chewing like a fool. I know how to catch him slipping and I know he got at least a quarter mil stashed away," Keishana informed him.

"Now you talking my language. Who is it?"

She looked up into his eyes for a couple of seconds before saying, "Your ex Candace's boyfriend, SK."

Nicholas Lock

Chapter 7

The saying was true: when it rains, it pours. After leaving Keishana's house last night, he drove around trying to get his mind together. She had hit him with a huge blow. Didn't nobody know it for a fact, but they all suspected Taz wanted Candace back, and that's exactly what he had in mind before Keishana dropped that bomb on him last night. He just wondered if she knew the nigga SK had one foot in the grave and if it was up to him, he was gon' help him put both in. The news really had Taz in his feeling. Even though Candace had done some real live bullshit while he was locked up, he still didn't want to see her in harm's way. But you reap what you saw, you do dirt you get dirt. He had reached out and got her number because he had to make she knew her nigga won't living right.

"Hello?" she answered, and just hearing her voice caused his heart to tighten up.

"Where you at?"

"Oh my God, hey! I'm at the house, why?"

"Meet me at our spot," he said, and then he hung up, not giving her a chance to answer.

Their spot was the Olive Garden. It was where they had met at. She was working as a waitress and he was there with his sister. As soon as he saw her, he knew he had to have her. It took a few weeks, but he finally got her to go out with him. He convinced her to quit her job and move in with him, and from then on, they were inseparable. They were trying to start a family when Taz got locked up. But after he got his time, their picture perfect romance ended.

Taz walked into the Olive Garden and got a booth in the corner where he could see the door. When Candace walked in, he stood up and waved her over.

"Damn, I can't get no hug?" she asked.

He just sat back down and she followed suit upon seeing she wasn't going to get one.

"So what did you call me here for?" she asked, salty about his icy reception.

"Before I go into all that, let me ask you a question. Why did you do that bird-ass shit?"

"First of all, I ain't do shit! You just jumped to conclusions. If you would have listened instead of hanging up, then you would've known that somebody broke into the house and took everything. They even took your clothes."

"Why you ain't just tell me all that?"

"I tried! But you wasn't trying to hear me out."

Damn, Taz thought, *maybe I did jump to conclusions.* After hearing all the money he had put in work for was gone, he really wasn't trying to hear shit else. Did he push her into the arms of another nigga? If so, it was too late now. She was part of the walking dead crew.

"Maybe you did, maybe you didn't. Anyway though, the reason I needed to holler at you was to let you know SK not living right."

"What you mean not living right?"

"He got AIDS, and before you ask how I know, my homegirl said he gave it to her and when she told him, she said he told her it was her fault, she should've made him wear a rubber."

After hearing that, Candace just sat there with a blank look on her face, staring off into space.

"I figured I'd let you know 'cause I didn't want to see you get played like that. Set you up an appointment to get tested. You might be straight," he told her as she continued to look into space. He got up, kissed her on the forehead, and left her to her thoughts. In the meantime, Taz had issues of his own he had to go deal with.

***

PJ had come through with Gutta's old lady's address and Taz and Kiki were sitting in her Escalade waiting for her to come home. Their plan was to snatch her up and make her call Gutta to come over.

"Damn, where this hoe at?" Kiki was getting restless.

"Sit your impatient ass down."

This was just like old times, he and Kiki stalking a victim. He just had to make sure he kept her impulsive ass under control. She was quick to fly off the handle, especially when things weren't going her way.

"There she go right there." Keasha pointed to a red Challenger coming down the street.

They ducked down in their seats as she drove by and pulled into her driveway. Once she went into the house, they got out and walked up to the house. Taz stepped to the side as Kiki rang the doorbell. As soon as she opened the door, Kiki punched her in the face, causing her to fall back on the floor. When Taz stepped into the doorway, her eyes got big and she started pleading her case.

"I'm sorry! I was drunk that night, I didn't mean nothing by it."

"Bitch, shut up!" Kiki kicked her in the stomach, making her curl up in the fetal position.

Taz went and sat down in the kitchen and Kiki dragged the girl in and made her sit across from Taz.

"This can go however you want it to go. All you got to do is call Gutta and get him to come here, and we can act as if this never happened," Taz informed her.

"Okay."

She pulled her phone out and called Gutta on speaker phone. He answered on the third ring.

"What up, gal?"

Hearing the nigga's voice had Taz's temperature on a thousand. All he could think about was the bullet holes in his daughter's room.

"When you coming over here? I ain't seen you all week."

"Mi down in Miami right now, but mi gon' be back in a couple days."

"But ba-"

Taz snatched the phone out of her hands. "Well, well, well, Mr. Gutta, it seems as if we have ourselves a situation."

"Who dis?"

"The man you been looking for, let you tell it. But this is how it's going down: I'ma borrow your little girlfriend right here until you return, and whe-"

"Nah, nah," Gutta chuckled, stopping Taz in mid-sentence. "Dat's not mi gal, pussy boi, more like mi whore. Mi don' care what you do wit' her."

"Fuck you, Gutta! You not shit! Take all his shit! It's in the den in the closet. How you like them apples, pussy!" the chick blanked.

Taz just hung up the phone because it was pointless to keep talking to him. He now had to decide what to do with this chick.

"Please don't hurt me, you can have all his stuff. Just take it and go," she pleaded as if reading his mind.

"What's your name?" Taz asked.

"Amanda."

"Okay, Amanda, this what's going to happen. We gon' grab Gutta's stuff and we gon' leave. I just need you to let this go. No police."

She nodded her head and told them where everything was at. It was $50,000 and a bird and a half. As Taz was loading the truck, he heard a gunshot go off in the house. His first reaction was to run in the house and check on Kiki, but he thought better of it. Instead, he just went ahead and got in the truck.

A minute later, Kiki came strolling out without a care in the world. When Kiki noticed they weren't moving, she looked his way and saw him staring at her.

"What, nigga?"

"I know you ain't do what I think you did."

"You know that dizzy-ass bitch couldn't wait to call the police. We not going to prison - not on my watch," she said, continuing to toy with her phone.

"You can't kill everybody," Taz told her, pulling out.

"Thank me later." She tossed the phone in his lap.

Taz picked up the phone and there was a picture of a mini mansion on the beach.

"Whose house is this?"

"Gutta's. He's a dummy. He got his phone registered to his name and address. The internet tells all," she said matter-of-factly.

"I guess we about to take us a trip to Miami," Taz said, making a mental note to change the address to his phone.

Nicholas Lock

Chapter 8

Taz and Kiki had made plans to go to Miami in two weeks. Kiki was handling all the minuscule details while Taz just waited for everything to fall in place. Once Gutta was dealt with, he was going to fall back and let Kiki, PJ, TK, and Reggie run shit. He was just going to take a backseat and raise his kids and try to make a son.

It had been a few weeks and the Mexican chick Isabella still hadn't called him, and he couldn't call her because he had lost her number. At the moment, he had some free time, so he decided to drop by and pop up on her. He put on a pair of Parish Nation jeans, a brown thermal, and some wheat Timberlands. His jewelry game was back on point. He had got a chain and had a charm made in the shape of the Tasmanian devil with blue diamonds for eyes. And he had replaced his presidential Rolex with another diamond-studded one. To top it off, he got his grill done in white gold with crushed diamonds all across the front.

"You did that," he told himself as he looked himself over in the mirror. He put on a couple dabs of Jean Paul Gaultier and was out the door.

When he pulled up to Micasita's, Isabella was outside talking on the phone. He parked and snuck up behind her and wrapped his arms around her.

"You just forgot all about me, huh?"

She jumped and tried to wiggle out of his arms, but he held her tighter.

"Let me go," she demanded in her sexy accented voice.

"Not until you tell me why you never called me. Damn, you smell good, girl."

"The same reason you ain't called me, now let me go!"

"You feel too good. Aw shit!" Taz doubled over from her

elbow to the stomach.

"I told you to let me go," she said triumphantly as Taz tried to catch his breath.

"I'm going to let that slide," he said, regaining his composure. "And the reason I ain't call you was because I lost your number."

"And I had to get a new phone, as you can see." She held up a new iPhone.

"Well, this what's about to happen: you about to go clock out and we about to go on our date right now."

"Not dressed like this, I'm not," she said, referring to her work uniform.

"Baby girl, you gon' look beautiful no matter what you wear. Now go get your stuff and come on," he said, causing her to blush.

After Taz's last statement, she went in to clock out and grab her things while he waited outside. While Taz was standing around waiting for her to come back out, a black Yukon pulled into the parking lot and parked. After a few minutes passed and nobody got out, he went on alert. Taz tried to see behind the tint, but it was useless. He turned his back to the truck and acted like he was reading the restaurant sign as he flipped the clip off his holster just in case. When Isabella came out, Taz grabbed her hand and led her to his car, all while keeping an eye on the truck.

"So what kind of food do you like to eat?" Taz inquired.

"I like all foods, but I really love seafood and Asian food."

"Shit!" Taz said seeing the Yukon pull out behind him.

"What?" Isabella asked.

"Nothing, but I have to take a raincheck on our date," he continued to keep an eye on the Yukon.

"Are you serious? I just left my job early, and now you say

it was for nothing. Just drop me off and never talk to me again." Isabella sat back and folded her arms across her chest.

Damn, Taz thought to himself. He didn't want to lose her before he even got her, but keeping her with him was out of the question. Damned if he did, damned if he didn't. It was only a matter of time before the Zoe Pound niggas started to open fire, and he didn't want to put Isabella in harm's way.

"Look, ma, I got some other shit going on and I'm not trying to put you in harm's way. You see that black truck behind us? It's been following us, and I think it's these dudes I been beefing with," he informed her.

"Harm's way? I'm from Mexico, I grew up in harm's way. And if you not man enough to protect me, then you do need to leave me alone. Besides, I can take care of myself if need be." She pulled a chrome .380 out of her purse.

Taz didn't know whether to be offended or what. Did she not understand by dropping her off he was trying to protect her?

"Pull over," Isabella said, eyeing the truck, which was still following them

"Yeah, when I get you somewhere safe."

"Just pull over at the gas station real quick."

"Fuck it." He pulled into the gas station.

As soon as he parked, she hopped out and started walking towards the truck.

"Stupid-ass bitch," Taz mumbled, drawing his hammer and rushing to catch up to her.

He caught her and spun her around. As soon as he did this, the doors to the Yukon busted open. Taz was getting ready to squeeze, but Isabella grabbed his arm and started speaking rapid Spanish towards the truck as four Mexicans piled out. They shared a brief exchange before she looked to Taz and told him that it was her brother. He walked back to the truck as she went to talk to her people.

"He said he apologizes, he didn't know who you were," Isabella stated as she climbed back inside.

"It don't even matter," Taz said, swinging his dreads out his face.

"Now where you taking me?"

"I should take your retarded ass back where I got you, and let me see that gun," he demanded, not quite sure how to take her. He checked the gun and saw it was loaded with one in the head. "You know how to use it?" He handed it back.

"Point and shoot, duh." She smirked.

"Yeah. A'ight."

They rode the rest of the way silent, in their own thoughts. Taz still felt like she had questioned his manhood with that if he couldn't protect her comment, but he was going to let it go for now and try to salvage their date.

Since she said she liked Asian food, he was taking her to Miyabe's, an open grill Japanese spot where they cooked the food right at the table.

"Oh my gosh! I been wanting to come here." She was excited.

They went inside and got a table in the back. They only bad thing about Miyabe's to Taz was the fact that you might be at a table with eight other people that you didn't know. Isabella took it in stride and they started getting to know each other while the chef cooked their food.

"So, Mr. Taz, what do you do for a living and why are you beefing with these people you're worried about?" She looked at him, placing her chin on her hands.

He just looked at her, trying to figure out just how much to tell her.

"First of all, I'm not worried about them. I was worried about you. And the beef stems from an incident that happened years ago. I work at Smithfield." Taz neglected to go into details.

"And what was the incident?" She wasn't giving him a break.

"Check it, I'm going to keep it short. I killed one of their homeboys and now they want some get back. You happy?"

"So you a killer?"

"Enough about me. Tell me about Ms. Isabella."

"Okay, you already know I'm twenty-one. I grew up in Guadalajara, Mexico. My mom got killed when I was a baby, so my dad raised me and my brother, if you want to call it that. So my aunt really raised us, but by the time I was fourteen and my brother Juan was seventeen, we were running the streets, raising ourselves. It started getting too dangerous, so my dad felt the need to send me over here, and here I've been for the last five years."

"What's your last name?"

"Vasquez, nosy."

Their conversation paused as they got their food. As they ate, Taz couldn't help but admire her beauty. Isabella had a natural beauty. She was pretty without trying to be. There was something else there; Taz just couldn't put his finger on it. She kind of reminded him of Kiki.

"It's impolite to stare." She caught him looking at her.

"I can't help it. Your ass so pretty. I got a question though. If your dad only sent you here, what is your brother doing here?"

"Juan comes and goes. Honestly, I'm surprised he even let me go with you or that he didn't at least didn't come say something. He's really, really overprotective. So where you taking me next?"

"You got somewhere in mind?"

She just shrugged her shoulders. They bagged the rest of

their food up and left.

Before she could get in the car, he grabbed her and turned her around to face him. Taz reached up and took her hair out of the bun, letting it fall, and just as he expected, it fell to the top of her ass. Taz pulled her into him and tilted her chin up, forcing her to look him in the eyes. Taz leaned down so his lips were inches from hers. They just stared at each other until she took the initiative and kissed him. Taz picked her up and she wrapped her legs around his waist as they continued kissing.

"Y'all need to get a room," someone said.

Taz turned ready to blank on whoever it was that wasn't minding their business, but Isabella beat him to it.

"Bitch, you need to mind your fucking business!" Isabella amped. Taz was starting to smile until he saw who it was.

"Whoa, whoa, whoa," Taz said as Kiki hopped out of her truck.

"I'm about to put this little hoe in her place." Kiki tried to get past Taz. As he was trying to hold Kiki back, he saw Isabella reaching inside her purse.

"Hell no!" he yelled as Isabella drew her .380

"Oh no this bitch didn't," Kiki calmly said and he saw Kiki's eyes get that little gleam in them. He knew if he let her go, she was gon' kill Isabella.

"This my little sister, Isabella, get your ass in the car."

"You need to teach the hoe some manners then," Isabella said and then got in the car.

Once she was in the car, Taz let Keasha go.

"You know she dead, right? And you need to tighten up on your surroundings. What if I would've been them Zoe Pound niggas? They not gon' greet you with words. It's gon' be bullets," she said, her words ringing true.

"I got you, and leave her be. I'm gon' set her straight.

Where you was headed?"

"On my way to the west side, but I seen your car and you out here fucking in the parking lot. Oh, and be ready Friday. We got a flight to catch," she said, walking back towards her truck.

Before she got in, she turned Isabella's way, made a gun with her hand, pointed it at Isabella, and pulled the trigger. As Kiki pulled off, Taz walked back to the car, trying to figure out how he was going to dead this beef between Isabella and Kiki before bloodshed happened. And the way it was looking, he was going to have to do it sooner rather than later.

Nicholas Lock

Chapter 9

Taz and Keasha boarded their flight that Friday at nine in the morning. He hadn't been around Kiki since the run-in with Isabella. He'd had to go through hell and high water to get Isabella to calm down. It took buying her a pair of Red Bottoms to get her halfway calm. Since then, they had gone on three more dates, and all of them ended with him not getting any pussy. But he was breaking her down, slowly but steadily. Plus he liked the fact that she wasn't an easy fuck. As long as he kept her and Kiki separated, he was straight.

"Where your bean eating-ass girl at?" Kiki tried being funny once they were seated.

"Aye yo, watch your mouth. She might turn out to be your sister-in-law."

"Hmm, I've never seen a wedding and a funeral at the same time. You'd go from husband to widower all in a couple hours," she stated while adjusting her seat.

Laughing, he said, "You a sick child, Kiki. But for real though, I'ma need you to let her live. Do it for me. I'm really feeling her," he admitted.

Kiki looked at him out the corner of her eye before saying, "You know what? Just because I love you, I'm going to give the hoe a chance. But you better keep her in check, because I ran out of my slap a bitch medicine."

Taz busted out laughing at his road dog.

"Oh yeah, bro. PJ, Reggie, and TK done took off. They eating like a fool, so much so that we gon' need to find a plug or something. Speaking of plugs, I think I got us a meal ticket lick. You know I been fucking around in Atlanta, and it's this crew down there that got the city on smash. They call them OTF. It stands for Only the Family. I got this bitch on the inside that fucks with one of the top niggas. She be feeding me all this information, not knowing no better. The whole crew is related, and the head dude is an older cat named Marvin. Matter of fact, here's a picture of him." She passed him her phone.

He was looking at a short, block-ass nigga with a brush cut. He kind of favored the rapper Akon. You could tell he had some age on him by the grey coming in around his temples, plus he wasn't dressed like a young nigga. He had on some tan slacks, a brown turtleneck, and some brown loafers. The only jewelry he wore was an iced-out watch and a pinky ring.

"Is this broad reliable?" Taz asked, giving her phone back.

"I mean, for the most part, yeah. Like I said, she don't know no better. She thinks I'm just a regular hood bitch."

"And what made her tell you all her business like that?"

"She a gossip queen, and I let her eat my pussy one night and she been hooked ever since."

"Whore," Taz joked.

"Anyway. She been telling me how her nigga been begging her for a threesome and she wanted to know if I'm down."

"Go ahead and set that shit up. You already know the routine."

"Okay, but it's gon' have to be mapped all to a T because it's not gon' be at no hotel. It's gon' take place at his house. You need to be on your shit because you know I'll go ahead and kill him before I let him put his dick in me."

"That's your problem, I think. You just want to let these niggas eat your pussy and not get no dick. That's why your ass be so mean." Taz leaned his seat back. "Matter of fact, is you still a virgin?"

"Shut up!" Kiki punched him in the arm "And for your info, no I'm not a virgin. I got my cherry popped while you were gone," she admitted loudly, causing an older while lady to hear her and turn red in the face.

"To who?"

"Damn, nosy."

"Don't get fucked up, little girl."

"Make your mind up, nigga! One minute you want me to fuck, then the next you get mad when I say I did. Indecisive-ass nigga."

"You know what? It don't even matter. Wake me up before we land," he said and then closed his eyes, letting her know the matter was closed.

"Nigga act like he my fucking daddy," Kiki mumbled to herself before trying to take a nap herself.

After their plane landed, they headed straight to the Trump Hotel, where they had booked a double room.

"I might have to move down here. It's in the forties back home, but here it's mid-seventies. I could get used to this," Taz said watching a group of women stroll by in booty shorts and bikini tops.

"You just want to come down here and be a hoe," Kiki said.

Taz ignored her as he walked inside the Trump Hotel and had to double take at the elegance of it all. But then again, he hadn't expected much less since they were paying almost half a bond a night. He could only imagine what a penthouse suite would cost. Upon further notice, he realized he was the only person in jeans and a wife beater and there was not one dread head in sight. But Taz didn't give a fuck. They got their key cards and proceeded to the room.

"Damn, nigga, act like you been somewhere before," Kiki said, brushing past him into the room.

Everything in the room looked expensive. The bedspread even looked like it cost a few bands. There was a full bar in the room that was fully stocked, a 60 inch glass plasma TV -

something Taz had never seen before - a sunroof and a big bay window that looked out over the city.

"I'm going to change real quick, then we can dip," Kiki said, and when Taz turned around to tell her to hurry up, he saw she was bent over digging in her suitcase ass naked.

Her walking around naked had never bothered him before. He never looked at her in that sort of way. But seeing her pussy poking out like it was with her slim waist and fat ass had his dick on rock solid.

"Go put on some fucking clothes!" he yelled, more mad at himself for his reaction.

She just brushed him off and continued looking in her suitcase. He just turned around and went back to looking over the city, asking himself what was the difference from any other time he'd seen her naked. Taz just concluded that it was most likely the fact that he hadn't had any pussy since the night he and Mary had fucked. She had been trying to get back up with him for a repeat, but he kept putting her off. She was starting to try to get a little too clingy and he didn't want her getting the wrong impression. She'd get the message sooner or later.

His phone interrupted his thinking. "What's up, bae?" he asked, seeing it was Isabella.

"Hey papi, what you doing?" She sounded sexy as ever.

"Down here waiting on Kiki to get done changing so we can handle some business."

"Papi, don't get in no trouble, because I got something special for you when you get back," she said, causing him to get excited.

"Is it wet and pink?"

"Oh my gosh. Stop being nasty, D'angelo!"

"Anyway, what kind of panties you got on?" he continued.

"Not telling you," she teased.

"Whenever you get done having phone sex, I'm ready"

Keasha said from behind him.

He turned around to see she was fully dressed and checking the clips to her .10mm's.

"Bae, I'm going to call you when I get done."

"Okay, bye, papi, and remember what I said."

"Got you. Let's go."

When they got outside, Kiki walked to a burnt orange Lamborghini Huracán and opened the door.

"Ain't no way you went and rented the most conspicuous car you could find. Nah, take it back and get a Honda or an Audi or something," Taz said.

"And how conspicuous are they gon' be in a neighborhood where the lowest priced house is two and a half million dollars and the only cars you see are Bentleys, Aston Martins, and Rolls Royces?" she said with her brow raised.

"You got that, but I'm driving." He had to win somewhere.

When they pulled into the neighborhood, Taz saw firsthand just what Kiki had been talking about. Every single house he passed was huge and had a foreign car in the garage or driveway. They pulled into a house three doors down from Gutta's house and parked. If someone came out, they were just going to say they were lost. As they watched his house, waiting for an opportunity to pounce, a black Suburban pulled up to Gutta's house.

"That definitely don't belong over here," Kiki said, pulling out her phone and pointing it in the direction of the SUV.

Taz's heart dropped when he saw who stepped out of the Suburban. He'd never forget that face as long as he lived. When Gutta stepped out on the porch and shook the man's hand and led him into the house, Taz immediately drove off as fast as he could.

"What the fuck is you doing?" Kiki asked, confused.

"That was Detective Evans, Kiki, and he's a fucking Fed."

Nicholas Lock

Chapter 10

After calming his nerves, he explained to Keasha that Detective Evans was one of the agents who busted in Quadress's house that night. He was the lead detective. He questioned Taz that night, but Taz kept talking him in circles.

"You know what, bro? This might work out in our favor. It's clear this detective Evans and Gutta have a personal relationship, but I'm curious to know do the top niggas in Zoe Pound know?"

"I see where you're going with this, but first we have to find out who the top man is, and second, how do we get him to talk to us? We can't be on his list of friends."

"It can't be too hard. You're on the Zoe Pound's most wanted list, so if you show your face in little Haiti, maybe he'll show up."

"Before or after they cut my head off? Sorry, but I think I want to live a little bit longer. But I do have an idea. How about we follow Gutta? Sooner or later he's going to have to meet with him, and when he does, we make our move. In the meantime, I'm going to enjoy this Miami weather."

They went back to the hotel, where he changed into a pair of swim trunks and got ready to hit the beach.

"Kiki, braid my hair for me," he said through the door that separated their rooms.

"Come on."

Taz walked into her room and Kiki was in the mirror pulling her hair into a ponytail.

"You not going nowhere with me dressed like that," Taz told her.

Kiki was wearing a white two-piece bikini that showed off every inch of her body. A regular bikini would've been okay, but this was anything but regular. The top was alright, but it was the bottoms that he didn't care for. They were basically a string that was all the way in the crack of her ass and the front barely covered her pussy. Plus he could tell by the fabric that when the water hit it, it was going to be see through.

"I'm grown," she said, sitting on the bed, allowing him to sit between her legs so she could braid his dreads back.

"You grown, but I ain't trying to have a bunch of niggas staring and trying to holla while I'm around."

"Deal with it, nigga, because I'm not changing," Kiki said forcibly.

Taz just left it alone because he really wasn't in the mood to go back and forth. She was just trying to be picky now, he knew. Taz had other more important issues to worry about than what Kiki wore. He still had to figure out what he was going to do about finding a plug for his team. Last time he talked to them, the word he got was that everybody was taxing on the work. If the ATL move turned out to be legit, then that would put them ahead of the game for some months. If everything went according to plan, he'd be rid of the headache that the Zoe Pound niggas were giving him, then he would hit the Atlanta crew. That would put him and everybody else in a good position and he'd be able to get back to spending quality time with his girls, something he hadn't been able to do ever since this beef had sprung up. The more time he spent in Miami, the more he was beginning to think this was going to be the place he raised his family.

"What you thinking about?" she asked, finishing up on his braids.

"Damn, I can't even have my thoughts to myself?" Taz joked.

"Come up off it," Keasha continued.

"Just thinking about what I'm going to do when all this is over with. I think I'm just going to handle this last bit of trouble we got and move down here with my girls and maybe Isabella - if she act right, that is." He got up and sat beside Kiki.

"I ain't nowhere in that equation, huh?" She looked him in the eyes.

Taz started laughing. "Aww, you feel left out," he joked. "Girl, you know damn well wherever I'm at, you gon' be too. You can stay at the house too. I don't know how Isabella gon' act, but fuck it. Now come on, let's hit this beach."

"Okay, give me a minute."

Taz went ahead and left to wait in the hallway. When Kiki came out, he saw she had put on a pair of jean booty shorts with the zipper open. Taz nodded his head in approval until she walked past him and he saw the back was cut so that the bottom of her ass was hanging out. He just shook his head.

They went to the beach and had a ball. You would've thought they were kids the way they were acting. They were dunking each other, playing Marco Polo. They even built some sand castles.

"I'm hungry as hell," Taz said, walking out of the water.

"Me too. I seen this Jamaican restaurant right down the street I want to try out. I'm dying for some curry chicken," she said, wringing her hair out.

"Lead the way."

As Taz was following Keasha off the beach, he couldn't help but notice the way her hips flared out from her nonexistent waist. Even in the shorts she wore, her ass was still moving like it had a mind of its own.

"Body like that, I know," she bragged, looking back and seeing him staring.

"Anyway, little girl. You better be glad you my little sister."

She rolled her eyes and slowed down so she could hold his

hand. They strolled down the street hand in hand, taking in the Miami atmosphere, lost in their own thoughts. As they approached the restaurant, a grey commercial van pulled up alongside of them and four dread heads jumped out with assault rifles and forced them in the van. Kiki got hit with the butt of a gun as reward for trying to get away. The van swerved off once they were in.

"Mi gone have fun wit' ya," one said, grabbing one of Kiki's breast.

Immediately, Taz lashed out with his foot, catching him full on in the mouth, knocking him to his ass. A blow to the back of the head caused Taz to fall to the floor of the van, and the second blow rendered him unconscious.

When Taz came back to, Kiki was cradling his head in her lap. When she saw his eyes open, she said "Oh my God, boy, you scared the shit out of me. I tried to wake you up, but you wouldn't. Don't do no more stupid-ass shit like that again!"

"My head hurts and you making it worse with your whining," he said, sitting up. "Where we at?" He looked around the room they were in.

"Some warehouse. They put us in here and ain't been back yet."

"You good?" he asked, standing up and trying to shake off the wooziness.

"Yeah, after you kicked dude in the mouth, they left me alone, for the most part."

Taz looked her in the eyes to make sure she wasn't keeping anything from him. Satisfied with her answer, Taz started looking for a way out of the situation they were in. They had left their guns and phones in the room, so that left him with few options. He tried the door, but as expected, it was locked.

"Come here," Taz told Keasha. "I'm going to lift you up to that window so you can tell me where we at." He picked her up and put her on his shoulders.

"Taz, all I see is more warehouses and the ocean."

"See if you can open it."

"It won't move," she said dejectedly.

"Fuck it." He put her down. "Look, I'm not going out like this, ain't no way! If I got to go, it's gon' be like a motherfucking gangsta! So check this: when they get ready to open the door, you stand to that side and I'ma rush them, gun or not. While that's going on, hopefully you'll be able to slide out, but I'm gone try to get my hands on one of them hammers."

"I'm not leaving you!"

"For one time in your fucking life listen, Keasha! I don't know where you getting this gung ho shit from, but ain't nothing cool about dying."

"Nigga, fuck that! Whatever happens to you gon' happen to me! You the only family I got, nigga!" she yelled, pointing a finger in his face. "I don't even know my parents because they got locked up and my pervert of an uncle took me in, and after you deaded him, it's just been you, motherfucker. Bonnie and Clyde, nigga! Without you, there is no me. Now stop talking stupid and let's figure out how to get out of this shit."

As soon as Kiki got done talking, the door swung open and ten Haitians rushed the room with Chiappas and Mac 90's. When Taz saw the one that grabbed Keasha, he immediately clenched his fist.

"Come on, mi bossman wants to see ya, an no funny business, boi. Dis time mi shoot ya," he warned Taz.

They led them out of the room and down a long hallway until they came to the main part of the warehouse. There were five white BMW M5's parked about the warehouse and on the hood of one sat a light-skinned dude with a brush cut. You could tell by his aura that he was in charge.

"You got some big balls, rude boi, coming down here to mi city after ya killed mi nephew," he said, confirming what Taz thought.

"He was a fucking rat!" Taz spat.

"Ya killed him and ya disrespect his honor. I've kilt people fa way less, boi," he stated calmly. "But mi a businessman. Mi son say he told ya dat ya had to pay an ya say fuck him."

"Gutta your son? Aww, man, do chasse eaters run in your family or something? Because your bloodline is fucked up!" Kiki said.

"Ya tongue is a powerful ting. It has the power over life and death, and yours is leading ya to a shallow grave."

Taz gave Kiki a look and she closed her mouth.

"You can keep your threats to yourself, but as far as Quadree and Gutta go, they're no good. And this isn't us just talking. We can back this up with facts. In my motion discovery, it had that Quadree was a federal informant, and we just took some pictures of your son Gutta shaking hands with an FBI agent. As for me paying you for killing a rat, ha, picture that! I just paid you with some sound information. Anything else is nonnegotiable."

"Mi don't tink you in a position to say what's negotiable."

"Maybe, maybe not. I'm prepared to die, so there's really nothing you can do to me."

"Ya got balls, mi a give ya that. Dis what mi do. Ya have two days ta prove what ya say is true. Afta dat, mi kill everything ya love," he said, opening the door to one of the M5's.

"And how do we find you, and what the fuck is your name?" Kiki asked, getting her tongue back.

"I'll find ya, and names aren't important."

With that, he pulled out with all his goons in tow.

Taz locked eyes with the dread head he had kicked in the

back of the van and winked. The next time they crossed paths, it was going to be bloodshed.

Nicholas Lock

Chapter 11

Taz and Kiki got on the next flight out of Miami International. They got back to Fayetteville late Saturday. Kiki went to get the pictures printed off her phone while Taz went home to get his motion discovery. The only problem they were going to have was that they had to wait to be contacted. They promised themselves when the Zoe Pound did come calling, they were going to be prepared. They bought some bulletproof vests and extra clips. Taz refused to be put in a situation where he was at someone else's mercy again. He didn't like the fact that the Zoe Pound had the upper hand. He hadn't felt like that since he was standing in front of the judge waiting to be sentenced. It was a feeling he told himself he wasn't going to feel again, but here he was. One thing about it, he was going to see to it that he got his get back one way or the other.

While they waited, Taz and Kiki decided to grab something to eat. They opted for Texas Roadhouse.

"What you getting?" Kiki asked, sliding into the booth across from him.

"A steak and a loaded potato. I'm glad to see you stepped your dress game up." Kiki had on some Gucci skinny jeans, a pink Gucci T-shirt, a Gucci jean jacket, and a pair of pink and white Gucci flats.

"Nigga, my dress game be on point, I just be choosing not to dress up all the time. A lot of shit don't be leaving me with a spot to put my fire."

"And that do?" he asked, looking her over.

Kiki pulled her jacket back, showing Taz her shoulder holster that held twin .45's and raised her brows.

They kicked it for a while, just shooting the shit, waiting for their food. As soon as their food arrived, Taz's phone started ringing.

"Hello."

"Oh Taz!" Candace cried. "I got HIV!" she sobbed in his ear.

Taz's heart broke. In the back of his mind, he knew there was a chance she might not have contracted the virus and he'd had his hopes up, but her revelation had killed all that. Fuck letting SK live. He had just worked his way up to getting shot on sight.

"Candace, calm down, it's gon' be okay," he tried consoling her.

Kiki rolled her eyes after hearing Taz say Candace's name. "You a sucker," she mouthed to him.

"It's not gon' be ok! Then this bitch-made nigga had the nerve to say 'oh well', like it wasn't no big deal. Taz, come over here." She continued to cry.

"I'm in the middle of something and I'm not coming to that nigga's house."

"This my fucking house! Taz, if you ever loved me, you'd come over here, I really need you," Candace begged.

She said the only words that could really touch him. He hated for his love to be questioned.

"I'm on the way," he told her and hung up.

"I see she still got a piece of you." Keasha shook her head. "Hurry up and get done with the hoe so we can be ready if these niggas call," she said, grabbing the steak off his plate.

Taz walked out of the restaurant with a lot on his mind. He got in his CT6 and proceeded to Candace's house. He didn't have too far to go since she stayed ten minutes from the restaurant. He sat in the car an extra five minutes after he got to her house, mentally preparing himself to deal with Candace. Taz adjusted his vest and got out of the car. Before he could knock, she opened the door and let him in. Just looking at her,

Taz could tell she was going through some shit. Her eyes were puffy and red from crying and her usually done up hair was disheveled.

"I'm so sorry, D'angelo."

"For what?" Taz asked, confused.

"For not being there. If I would've been there for you while you was in prison, I probably wouldn't be going through this." she started crying again.

"Candace, stop beating yourself up, you good, I ain't tripping."

"I'm not good! I'll probably be dead in a couple months," Candace lamented.

"Nah, you just got to take care of yourself. Magic Johnson been living with HIV for years now." He tried giving her some hope.

"I don't want to talk about it. That's not why I called you over here. I need your help," she said, grabbing his hand and leading him through the house and up the steps. When they got to her bedroom door, Taz stopped and said, "Nah, Candace, we not about to do that."

"Nigga! I would never try to play you like that! Now come on." She led Taz into her bedroom and said, "This is what I need your help with."

"Oh shit!" Taz said, looking at the bed where a dead SK lay.

"He was talking crazy, acted like he ain't give a fuck about giving me no disease. Then he had the nerve to say how he was going to kill you. So I grabbed his gun and told him that I never stopped being your bitch. Then I shot him," she admitted.

"Damn, how many times you shoot him?" Taz looked around at all the shell casings by the bed.

She just shrugged her shoulders nonchalantly.

"What you want me to do, Candace?" He looked over at her.

"Get him out of here!"

"Huh?" Taz just looked at Candace. He pulled his phone out and called Kiki and told her to come over to Candace's house ASAP.

"Bring your ass over here and help me because this is your problem!"

Taz got her to help wrap SK up in the bed sheets and set him on the floor. As he got a chance to sit back and think, the magnitude of the situation really dawned on him. He was in his ex's house with her dead boyfriend wrapped up in some sheets. This was a lengthy prison sentence waiting to happen. Why did he always find himself in these fucked-up situations? The only good thing he could get from this was that he no longer had to worry about SK. But the one thing that was messing with his mind was where Candace got this gangster from. Taz used to have to make her shoot his gun. She was so bougie; it didn't make no sense. If she so much as broke a nail, it was the end of the world. So where she got the balls to kill a nigga was beyond him. He made a note to keep an eye on her from this point on. The doorbell ringing brought him out of his thoughts.

"Go get the door, don't just stand there" Taz told her while trying to figure out what he was going to do with SK's body.

"Nigga, what the fuck is it that you had me rush over here and-" Kiki started saying until she saw the body on the floor. Then she looked from Taz and Candace and back to Taz.

"Don't look at me, this her handiwork."

"Bravo. About time you put your big girl panties on."

"Yo, y'all sitting here like it's not a dead body in the room. We need to get this took care of first, then I don't care what y'all do."

"What's the plan?" Kiki asked.

"I don't really got one," Taz admitted.

"Let's just dump him in the river and be done with it. We got more important issues to be worried about," Kiki reminded him.

Taz just looked at Kiki. She always had that ruthless mentality, but since he had come home, she had been downright cold-hearted.

"What?" Kiki asked.

"Nothing. Just come on."

They wrapped SK in some more blankets and put him in the trunk of his car. He told Candace he was going to catch her later and pulled off to get rid of SK. As he was turning off her street he saw Kiki get back out and go back into Candace's house. Knowing their previous history, he hoped Candace made it out alive.

After dumping SK in the Cape Fear River, he was headed back through downtown on his way to meet Kiki when a red Camaro pulled up alongside of him. When he looked, he saw the top dog of the Zoe Pound, and when they locked eyes, he motioned for Taz to pull over. Taz pulled into the parking lot for the 82nd Airborne Museum and hopped out. Thinking he was by himself, Taz was going to kill him until the four other Camaro's pulled in behind him. This meeting was going to be different. They were on his home field, so the deck was stacked in his favor.

"I got all the information you wanted, but my question is, just what do you plan on doing with it? If you don't plan on killing Gutta, then there's no point in giving it to you," Taz said as everyone got out their car.

"Mi see ya balls have gotten bigga since mi last seen ya," he stated.

"An mi don' have a problem cutting dem off," the dread head that had grabbed Kiki's breast spoke up.

"Try me, pussy!" Taz amped.

"Ya in no position to be aggressive, boi," the one with the brush cut said.

"I think I am," Taz said as Kiki, TK, PJ, and Reggie pulled in with ten other cars.

There were close to sixty people standing behind Taz when everyone pulled out of their cars. They had brought most of the city's heavy hitters out. He saw niggas from all sides of town. He saw Zay and his boys from the east side, Slick and his clique from the west side, Streets and his crew from the north, and the rest was his day ones from the south.

"You might want to rethink your last statement. Now I'm not going to be as inhospitable as you was while I was in your city and tie you up. But before we go any further, I need to know your name" Taz said.

"Zion," he conceded.

"Now after I give you this info, are you going to handle the situation appropriately?"

"It'll be handled accordingly."

Hearing that, Taz handed him the pictures and the statements about Quadree. After Zion looked everything over, he nodded his head.

"Ya no longa will have to worry about Gutta and the Zoe Pound. Our beef is done." He turned to walk away when a shot rang out.

The dread head that Taz had kicked in the van was lying on the ground grabbing his throat. When Zion turned around, instead of Taz holding a gun, it was Kiki.

"He told me he was going to rape me," she said, walking away.

Zion looked down at his comrade and got in his car and

swerved off, leaving him to die.

They waited until Zion and his people were gone before they pulled out. With all that taken care of, Taz was going to go pick his daughters up and relax.

Nicholas Lock

Chapter 12

Taz decided he was going to take a day off from all the mayhem and take a family day. He knew from experience that if he dealt in the streets day in and day out, it would become a part of him. So today, it was going to be all about his family. He was taking his daughters and his sister out to eat at the Olive Garden, then they were going to take his girls to Monkey Joe's, an indoor trampoline spot. He was keeping it simple today. He had just put on a black and purple track suit, some purple and black Foam Posits, and a purple and black Baltimore Ravens beanie.

"Somebody at the door, Daddy!" D'Azia yelled from the front of the house.

Taz made his way to the door, thinking it was Tyshae and Kiki.

"Shae why you bring the devil with you?" Taz asked, letting them in, and then he saw Kiki had two duffel bags in her hands.

"I didn't. She pulled up the same time I did, thank you very much."

"What, nigga, I ain't welcome?" Keasha questioned.

"What's in them bags, Kiki?" Taz ignored her question.

She nodded her head towards the back and he followed her, wondering what kind of scheme Kiki had up her sleeve. He shut the door to his bedroom and Kiki dumped the duffel bag out on his bed.

"Oh shit! Where you get all that?" he asked as Kiki spread the bricks out over his bed.

"When we helped your girl with SK, I got to thinking. Where was his work at? So I went back in and talked to Candace, and she took me right to it."

"How many is it?"

"Twenty-five."

The wheels immediately started turning in his head. That was enough to set TK and them straight for a minute and at the same time lace his pockets up. Candace had come through with the come-up.

"I already know what you thinking, and I'm on top of everything. I'm going to distribute them to PJ and TK, then use some bread to get some pounds for Reggie." Kiki had everything under control.

"Daddy!" Neveah busted in the room. "We waiting on you! Hey Kiki."

"What I tell you about just busting in my room before knocking?"

"Leave her alone! When we going to get our nails done again?" Kiki asked.

"Whenever my daddy let me." She put her hands on her little hips.

"Okay now, bye." Taz ushered her out his room.

"And we need to make a trip to the A in the near future so we can start setting things in motion," she reminded him.

"A'ight, bet. Now get them shits out my house." Taz was nervous with all the work in his house.

"Scary ass." She slung the duffel bags over her shoulder.

After getting rid of Kiki, Taz, his sister, and his girls set off to the Olive Garden.

"I heard about you too," Tyshae said.

"What?"

"Y'all out here acting stupid, shooting people and shit."

"Who told you that dumb shit, and why you got them big dumb-looking shades on?"

"It don't matter who told me, but you need to sit your ass down. And my shades look good, stop hating." Tyshae mushed him in the side of the head.

"Keep your hands to yourself." He mushed her back, causing her shades to fall off her head, revealing a black eye that was almost closed.

Taz slammed on brakes in the middle of the road. "I'm only going to ask you one time, Shae. What happened to your eye?"

Shae just sat there looking out the window, not giving him an answer.

"I'm not moving this motherfucking car until you tell me what's up with your eye."

"You said a bad word, Daddy." Neveah said from the back seat.

Taz just looked at his daughter and she shut up. The car behind them started blowing the horn. He ignored the car and just sat there. He had a good idea what happened, but he wanted to be absolutely sure.

"Me and Big Sean got into it, okay! Now drive," she admitted.

Taz knew it. Before he got locked, up he was going to kill Big Sean, but Tyshae had begged him not to. He told the nigga the last time they saw each other that if he put his hands on somebody he loved again, his mama had better make sure she had his life insurance policy paid up.

"That's who told you that too, ain't it?"

Her silence confirmed his suspicions. He wasn't going to mess up their family outing, so he was going to chill for the moment, but the minute he got a chance, Big Sean was a dead man. He texted Kiki a message, letting her know if she saw him to handle it. Neither of them said a word until they got to the Olive Garden. His daughters were even quiet since they knew he was in a bad mood.

"Don't do nothing stupid, D'angelo. I'm done with him, for real this time," she pleaded as they pulled into the parking lot.

"I already know," he said and got out.

The Olive Garden wasn't crowded, so they were able to be seated as soon as they walked in.

"What y'all rug rats want?" he asked his girls.

"I want some meatballs!" Neveah, the more animated of the two, yelled out.

"What about you, D'Azia?"

"Spaghetti and meatballs."

Taz ordered a lasagna and breadsticks while Tyshae ordered Chicken Parmesan.

"Can I have a phone?" D'Azia blurted.

He looked at Tyshae and balled his face up.

"What do a ten-year-old need with a cell phone?"

"Aunt Shae said she would get us one," Neveah chimed in.

Tyshae put her head down as Taz looked over at her.

"Oh, she did? Well tell her to buy, it because I'm not."

"I got y'all," Tyshae told them. "Oh yeah, bro, I got a business proposition for you too." She expertly changed the subject.

"What might that be?"

"I remembered you said something about going legit, and I've been thinking, you know, with me being manager at the bank, I get all the foreclosures across my desk and I know all the businesses that are in financial straits. I can get you first dibs on all of them and I'm telling you, you can make a nice piece of legal money off these. If done right, you'll be able to clear at least three to four hundred thousand annually, maybe more."

"And what exactly do I have to do?" His curiosity was piqued.

"Okay, listen, all the foreclosures come across my desk

first. I'll pick out the ones that have the highest profit margin and put them to the side. I'll get you a good price on them, then you can either sell them for a minor profit or you can upgrade them a little bit and make a major profit. Now with the businesses, you get them back on track and charge interest or you can give them the money and buy a stake in the business, which is what I suggest. That way, you'll continue to get paid throughout."

The whole time she was explaining, Taz was mentally calculating the amount of money he was willing to part with. He had already decided he was going to make the move after her first two sentences.

"And what do you get out of this?" Taz asked, taking a bite of lasagna.

"Getting you out of the streets and on the right path. Your girls need you and I need you, plus Kiki really needs you. When you left last time, she went crazy."

"I got you, I got you. I knew you wasn't gon' eat all that food." He snatched some meatballs off D'Azia's plate.

"When I go to work on Monday, I'll set everything in motion."

"Let's go, Daddy," Neveah whined.

"Why you always trying to tell me what to do?"

"'Cause she knew she can," his sister told him.

"Anyway."

Taz paid the bill and they left the Olive Garden, and at the moment, Big Sean was all forgotten about.

The whole ride to Monkey Joe's, his daughters were in the back seat, all hyped up about going there.

"Make sure y'all burn off all that energy inside, because when we get back home, I want y'all to take a bath and leave me alone," stated Taz as he pulled the CT6 into Monkey Joe's.

It was utter chaos when they walked inside the building.

There were kids all over the place ripping and running.

"This is why I don't have kids," his sister admitted.

"You know it's about that time. You not getting no younger. Twenty-eight ain't no spring chicken. I need me some nieces and nephews."

She just rolled her eyes and took off after D'Azia and Neveah. Good, Taz thought, now he didn't have to run behind them and it gave him time to call his boo. He found a seat away from all the ruckus and called Isabella.

"What?" she answered.

"Oh, that's how you gon' treat me?"

"I'm so done with you! You told me when you got back we was going to spend some time together. It's been a week!"

"You miss daddy, that's all you got to say. Baby, I really been tied up and right now, I'm out with my girls and Tyshae. But you have my word, in the next few days, it's gon' be just us. I quit my job so I'm going to have a lot more free time."

"If you don't, I don't ever want to hear or see you again."

Chuckling, he said, "You don't mean that. Why you so feisty all the time? I know exactly what your issue is. You need me to come stroke that kitty for you."

"I guess that's why I ain't never let you even smell this pussy," she teased.

"That's because you know when you do, I'm going to have you dick whipped," Taz boasted.

"Boy, boo!" She giggled. "Oh, and papi, I seen this Gucci dress that I'd look real good in."

"What you telling me for? Why you didn't buy it?"

"It cost $6500." She pouted

Taz smiled. He knew she wanted him to buy it. Truth be told, as he thought about it, every time they went out she was designer down. He had been meaning to ask her about that. She wasn't buying all that on no waitress salary.

"Baby, you know I got you, but I got a question. Where the hell you be getting all that other name brand stuff from?"

"My daddy. I'm the only daughter he has and I'm the baby."

"What he do?"

"He runs the biggest import/export business in South America. He mainly does business with the U.S. He was just in Washington D.C speaking to the president and Congress about the tariffs the president had just imposed," she stated proudly.

"Damn, excuse me, I might need to borrow some money one day then."

"You know I got you."

"Whatever, girl, but anyway, let me get back to these kids."

"Okay, and you better call me tonight too."

"Bye."

Taz went off in search of his girls and Tyshae because he was ready to go and if they weren't, he was going to call them an Uber because he was leaving.

Taz was tucking his girls into bed when Keasha called.

"What up, Kiki?"

"Turn on the news," she said, "and hurry up."

Taz went and turned the news on to see what she was talking about.

"This is Channel 11 news and we're outside of Lake in the Pines apartment complex, where authorities are investigating a gruesome murder. Hours ago, the body of Sean Turner was found in his car with several bullet wounds to his neck and facial area. Anyone with information should call 910-555-1500."

"That's my girl!" Taz said out loud. He would be able to rest much easier knowing big Sean wouldn't be able to hit his sister again.

Chapter 13

Taz was making good on his promise. He was on his way to pick Isabella up so they could spend some quality time together. Taz had planned a day in which he planned on pampering Isabella, but at the end of the day, he was getting that pussy no ifs, ands, or buts.

"You a whole live copycat. If I knew when I told you what I was wearing you were going to copy me, I wouldn't have told you," Taz said as Isabella got in the car.

"Quit playing, you know we look cute together." She kissed him on the lips.

Taz had told her he was wearing some black Balmain jeans with the brown stonewashing on the front, a brown Ralph Lauren turtleneck, and a pair of wheat Timberlands.

"When did you dye your hair?" Isabella had put blond streaks in her hair.

"You don't like it?" she asked insecurely.

"Hell yeah I do, boo." Taz ran his hands through her hair.

"What we doing here?"

"Oh, you don't want that Gucci dress no more?"

"Come on!" She hurried up and got out the car.

Taz was shaking his head as he followed her into the Cross Creek Mall. She grabbed his hand as he caught up to her. As they walked Taz kept looking at her butt.

"Why you keep looking at my butt?"

"I don't know what you been doing, but that ass done got fat!"

Giggling, she said, "Baby, my booty been big. I just be wearing big pants because I got tired of dudes commenting on my body."

Taz couldn't front that may have been the case because her butt was almost as big as Kiki's, and that was saying something since Isabella was petite as hell.

As they were heading towards the store that had the dress she was so adamant about, he spotted Candace. She narrowed her eyes when she saw him and Isabella. She surprised him because instead of coming to where he was, she pulled out her phone and got to typing, so he knew he had a text coming. But he definitely wasn't ready for what it said.

Candace: So you fucking the plug's daughter? You better not hurt that little girl because he'll kill you for it. I know you and Kiki blow that smoke, but her daddy blow smoke and fire.

Taz: You tripping, her daddy in the import/export business. You got the wrong girl.

Candace: I know Isabella Vasquez when I see her. Yeah, he in the import/export business, but do you know what he mainly exports? I know because that was SK's plug.

She dropped a bomb on him with her last text. Taz just looked at Isabella as she looked over the dresses. He hoped she hadn't intentionally lied to him. Maybe she didn't know exactly what her dad did. But Taz instantly thought about the day her brother had followed them. The more he thought about it, the more he noticed little things he overlooked, like her saying she moved over here because Mexico had gotten too dangerous or the fact that she always carried that .380.

"What's wrong, baby? Why you looking like that?"

"Hurry up and pick the dress so we can dip, because we need to talk," he said seriously.

"Okay," she said with a puzzled look on her face.

She grabbed a red spaghetti strapped mini that put an $8,500 dent in his pocket. As they left the mall, Isabella kept looking at Taz, trying to get a feel for him because he hadn't said a word since he told her they needed to talk.

"What's wrong, Taz? Did I do something?" She was confused at his sudden display of silence.

"Nah," he said still trying to wrap his head around the news Candace had delivered.

She just sat back in her seat, seeing she wasn't getting anywhere with her questions. After another five minutes of riding in silence, she put her hand in his lap and said "Baby, please don't be mad at me."

"I'm not mad" he moved her hand.

In her mind, she thought he was mad because she had been playing the hard to get role as far as sex was concerned. So she put her hand back in his lap and pulled his zipper down.

"Move, Bella." He tried to move her hand, but she wasn't going for it.

"Just drive."

Isabella reached in his jeans and pulled his dick out. She leaned over and ran her tongue around the head, causing his to rock all the way up. She moved her hair out of the way and took him into her mouth and starting bobbing her head up and down. Taz grabbed a handful of her hair and started guiding her head while driving with one hand. Isabella got up on her knees and unbuckled her jeans, never taking her mouth off his dick. She then reached her hand inside her jeans and started playing with her pussy.

"Mmm," she moaned around his dick.

She pulled his dick out her mouth and jacked him off a few times before running her tongue from the base to the tip. Taz pushed her head back down, forcing her to take him to the back of her throat. He pulled her pants down over her ass and replaced her hand with his. She was dripping wet. He started pushing two fingers in her sex and she started to rock back and forth on his fingers.

"You gon' make me cum, baby," she said.

Taz pulled into Sandpiper's and parked in the back.

"Get your ass in the back and take them pants off."

Taz got out and got in the backseat. He had planned to wait until later on tonight to fuck her, but the plan went out the window when she started sucking his dick.

When Taz got in, Isabella was already butt naked and waiting. Taz pulled down to his knees and told her to sit on his lap. Isabella slid down on his dick with her back to him and began to rock back and forth. Taz sat back, watching as she took over their sexing. Isabella leaned forward, grabbed the front seat, and starting bouncing up and down aggressively.

"Slow down," Taz said, grabbing her hips.

"I'm about to cum, papi," she hissed as Taz reached around and toyed with her swollen clit.

Her pussy started gripping his dick tighter as she reached her climax.

"Fuck, papi!" she yelled, leaning back into Taz.

"Nah, you not getting off that easy."

Taz pushed her all the way over the front seat until her breasts were touching the center console. He repositioned himself so that he was on his knees and Isabella's legs were around his waist. Then he slid in until he hit the bottom.

"Oh shit, daddy!" Isabella moaned out.

As he slid in and out of Isabella's love box, she tried to reach her hand back to keep him from going so deep, but Taz wasn't having it.

"What's my name?" he asked as he sped his strokes up.

"Taz, Taz, Taz!" Isabella screamed, pulling her hair.

"Where you want this nut at?"

"Cum in me, papi, I want to have your baby."

Taz stuck his thumb in her butt and started giving Isabella

everything he had to offer. Isabella's love juices coated his wood as another orgasm rushed over her. Taz pushed all the way in as his seed spilled inside of Isabella. He slow stroked a few more times before pulling out and sitting back.

"You still mad at me, papi?" she asked, getting up and crawling in his lap.

"I was never mad. Watch out." Taz pulled his pants back up and helped her put her clothes on.

"So what you need to talk to me about?"

"We gon' talk about it after we get a table."

Taz made sure Isabella's clothes were up to par before they proceeded to the restaurant. Taz had to figure out how to breach the subject of her pops being the man. He had a little doubt, but Candace had never lied to him before. One thing for certain, he was about to find out everything he needed to know before they left.

Once they were seated, they went to the buffet line and Taz filled his plate up with everything from shrimp to hush puppies. Sandpipers was hands down the best seafood spot on the east coast, and they even had a drive through.

"Try this, papi," Isabella urged, pushing some sushi his way.

"I had enough of raw fish for today." He grinned

"Suit yourself. Wait a minute, what the fuck you mean?" Isabella threw her fork at him and he busted out laughing. "Laugh now, no chocha later."

"I don't care," he bluffed. "But look, I got to ask you something, and I need you to be truthful. What do your dad really do?" He looked at her, trying to judge her reaction.

She stopped eating and looked up at him.

"I told you already."

"Don't play with me, Bella. If I find out you lying to me, we over with," he warned.

"I'm not." But after a few minutes, she said, "Look, D'angelo, are you serious about us as a couple?"

"If I wasn't, I wouldn't be spending all this time and money on you."

"Okay, here's the deal. My daddy is a kingpin. He runs the Mexican Mafia. The restaurant where I work is mines. He bought it for me. I just be working so I can have something to do. I didn't want to tell you because I didn't want you to look at me differently," she confessed.

Taz sat there looking at her as she revealed her secret. He definitely wasn't upset. He was trying to figure out how he was going to capitalize off her revelation. It could be a blessing and a curse. A blessing because this could be the plug he needed to get his team on the path to riches. A curse because, from the information he had, he couldn't afford to hurt Isabella. He couldn't afford to go to war with her father. He didn't have the money or the manpower. He was going to have to make sure he kept Kiki mellow because regardless of who her father was, Kiki would have no qualms about putting Isabella in a coffin.

"Come on, boo, let's go." Taz got up.

"Where we going? I ain't finished eating," she complained.

"Put that shit in a doggie bag. We going home. I'm not done beating that back out."

"I thought you had enough raw fish today?" she asked, putting the rest of her food in the doggie bag.

"Changed my mind."

He led her out the restaurant while texting Kiki, telling her to call him tomorrow because he might've found them a plug.

Chapter 14

"Okay, here's the list of foreclosed homes and businesses that are in financial struggles."

They were in Tyshae's office at Wells Fargo going over her business proposition.

"I already highlighted the ones that I feel will have the highest profit margin. It's going to cost you a little change, but I promise you, it's going to be well worth it," Tyshae said.

"What's a little change?" Taz inquired while looking over the list.

"It really depends, but the lowest is thirty-five thousand. If I were you, though, I'd help Primo's Pizza and Weiner Works first. Primo's is sixty thousand in debt and Weiner Works is seventy-five thousand in."

"Hypothetically speaking, let's just say I did have that kind of money. If I were to just walk in with that kind of bread, the Feds would have my ass in jail ASAP."

"First off, nigga, this me you talking to. I'm willing to bet you got more than that stashed away and I checked your bank account before you got here, and you got sixty-five thousand in there. Fix your face, nigga, I'm not telling you to use it. I got everything mapped out. My homegirl is the chief loan officer and I got her to approve for you to get a loan for up to two hundred thousand. All you got to do is fill the paperwork out. Here she comes now," Tyshae pointed out.

Taz turned around as a tall blond chick entered the office. He looked her over and was fairly impressed. She was about 5'7", 125 pounds, and she had the typical white girl shape. She had D-cup breasts and an okay little booty, but her face looked like something out of a magazine. If Taz did the white girls, she would be a prime candidate.

"Hey, Allison! This is my brother D'angelo, he's the one

that's getting the loan."

"Oh, okay. Well, if you'll just follow me, we'll go ahead and get the necessary paperwork done and have you on your way."

Taz got up and followed her out. Taz was a man, so it was only right that he checked her out further as he walked behind her. The pencil skirt she wore had her little butt and hips looking real edible. And not only did she have a supermodel face, she had the rip the runway walk.

"Have you ever modeled before?" he answered when they got to her office.

"No, why do you ask?"

"You have the face and you got the walk down pat," he said truthfully.

She gasped. Her eyes got big, she covered her mouth, and turned bright red.

Taz started laughing at her reaction. "Chill, ma, it ain't that serious. I was just stating the obvious."

"No, no, it's just I've never had someone tell me that, and I'm going to tell Tyshae you were looking at my butt." She squinted her eyes.

"I'm her big brother, she can't tell me nothing. Besides, I don't think it's nothing wrong with admiring beauty," he said, causing her to turn red again. "So what papers do I have to sign?" He steered the convo in another direction before it got too risqué.

She gave him the papers and showed him where to sign and he was off back to Tyshae's office.

When he walked in, Shae was on the phone, so he just made himself comfortable on the sofa she had against the wall. She handed him the reports on Primo's Pizza and Weiner Works while still talking on the phone.

Taz looked over the info on Weiner Works first. They were

a local family-owned fast food spot that specialized in hot dogs. They offered burgers, fries, and milkshakes as well, but their signature was the footlong hot dog they offered. It was the longest hot dog in the U.S., but it was slimmer. Up until a few years ago, their profits were high, but as of late, they were taking a nosedive. Upon further inspection, Taz thought he might have a solution, and he was going to discuss it with the owners when he met them.

Next he checked Primo's out. They were also locally owned. They went from being one of the top five pizza places to the bottom half in a year and a half. Taz definitely couldn't figure it out because he had taken his daughters there plenty of times and he loved it. Primo's sold regular pizza, but what made them unique was the way their other pizzas were made. They were like burritos because the crust was surrounding all sides of the pizza and the inside was where the actual pizza was. You could pick whatever toppings you wanted. Just like with Weiner Works, Taz thought he saw a solution that would immediately raise the profit margin.

"You a piece of work, you know that?" his sister asked.

"Oh lord, what I done did now?"

"Leave Allison alone, that's what."

"Man, you know I don't even do the snowbunnies."

"That was her on the phone. She told me what you said, and I know you." Shae pointed at him. "She's been through enough. She just got out of an abusive marriage, and besides, she's old enough to be your mother," she continued to scold him.

"Shae, you wasting your breath. She not my type, plus she a bunny." Taz put emphasis on the word bunny. "And how old is she?"

"Forty-nine, she got a daughter that's twenty-five. And it ain't so much you, it's her. She was asking about you. Before you had came, we was talking about how she had never dated a black dude before. I told her you was absolutely no good, all you were going to do was leave her with a sticky mouth and a wet ass."

"You dumb as hell." He laughed.

"Oh, and I got you a meeting with Mrs. Barnes from Weiner Works and Mr. Tessatore from Primo's. You need to meet Mrs. Barnes at 2:30 and Mr. Tessatore at 5: 00. Don't wear that. Put a suit on or something."

"Yes, Mama." He got up.

They hugged and Taz left. He saw Allison standing in her doorway as he walked out. He nodded his head and kept it hot. *Maybe in another lifetime*, he thought as he got in his car.

Taz and the owner of Weiner Works were meeting at Golden Corral. When he got inside, he was led to the back, where they were sectioned off from the rest of the restaurant. Taz had chosen well with his attire. He wore some black Gucci stocks, a blue long-sleeved Gucci button up with some Gucci cuff links, a black vest, and some black Stacy Adams. He opted to leave the coat in the car. He was only expecting Mrs. Barnes, but there were two other women seated with her.

"How are you doing, Mrs. Barnes?" Taz reached out his hand.

She stood and shook his hand. Her grip was surprisingly strong for a seventy-five-year-old woman and her eyes didn't have that dull look that he was used to seeing in elderly people, they actually had a youthful look.

"I'm fine, Mr. Walker. These are my daughters, Olivia and Victoria. They have a stake in the business."

Taz looked the trio over. They were all redheads with green eyes. Olivia appeared to be the youngest of the daughters, but Victoria was the curvier one. They were all dressed in business attire: dark skirts and light blouses. The only difference was the daughters wore stilettos while the mom wore flats.

"Shall we get down to the matter at hand?" Mrs. Barnes got down to business.

"What exactly are you looking for in return for your money?" Victoria started the discussion.

Taz was thrown off a little bit because he didn't know exactly how to proceed. He didn't want to waste his time explaining his pitch to her if she wasn't the one making the decisions.

"Mr. Walker, my daughters are who I'm leaving my business to. They're really the ones running it. As of late, I've taken a backseat in the daily operation of the business. I'm just here more so as a buffer to make sure my daughters don't make any rash decisions. They're co-CEO's, so the decision of whether or not to take your money is mainly up to them." She read his mind.

"Here's the deal," Taz began. "At first, I just wanted to loan you the money and put some interest in it, but after looking over your financial statements for the last few years, I see potential, so what I'm looking for is a stake in the business and a voice," Taz said. But the look on Victoria's face told him no.

"What do you mean a voice?" Olivia asked.

"I feel as though I have some ideas that would help the business get back its profitable ways which would benefit all of us."

"No and no," Victoria said.

Olivia looked over at her mother as if for her opinion, but her face remained impassive.

"I say yes, and I don't know about the voice part," Olivia countered.

"You can't be serious, Liv," Victoria said. "Mom."

"I'm quite serious, unless you have the money you need to say yes."

They started to go back and forth.

"Enough! Both of you," their mom ended their bickering. "Mr. Walker, how much of a stake are you looking to get?"

"What are you all's stakes?" he came right back, causing her to look at him as if she was seeing him for the first time, then smiled.

"I control fifty percent and my daughters have twenty-five apiece."

"Being that you're going to step all the way down in the near future, that leaves Olivia and Victoria with fifty percent apiece. So a five percent stake will suffice for now, and when you retire, an increase to fifteen percent."

Mrs. Barnes sat back as if pondering his proposal as both her daughters looked at her to see what her response was going to be, which let Taz know who really made the decisions.

"Okay. I'll have my lawyers draw it up and have it ready for you in the morning." She got up, signaling that their meeting was over. He shook her hand as well as Victoria's and Olivia's on the way out.

"I look forward to working with you, and I can't wait to hear what you have planned that's going to make our profits go back up," Olivia said while shaking his hand.

"Me either." Taz could see his bank account growing right before his eyes.

Taz met with Mr. Tessatore at his home in Hope Mills, and they came to an agreement immediately in which Taz got thirty percent of the business.

Today was a good day, Taz thought to himself while leaving Mr. Tessatore's house. Now the only thing he had to do was finish up his business in the streets and watch the money pile up.

But as Taz knew, nothing ever went according to plan.

Nicholas Lock

Chapter 15

"Oh my God, I'm so nervous," Isabella said, looking over at Taz.

They were on their way to Micasita's, where Isabella had arranged for Taz to meet her father. At first, she straight up refused the idea, but after a lot of coaxing, fucking, and pussy eating, she finally relented.

"I'm more nervous than you," Taz told her.

"Not you, Mr. Tough Guy," she joked.

"Not for the reason you think. I'm more so nervous about how your daddy gon' act when I put you on the table and start eating you. That dress you got on is doing something to me."

"Stop being nasty, papi! At least wait until he leaves. Then you can eat this chocha on every table in the building." She ran her hand across his zipper.

The closer they got to the restaurant, the quieter Isabella got. She had told him she had never let any of her boyfriends meet her father. This was more than just a meet and greet. Little did she know he planned on trying to get him to supply him. Taz wanted his whole team rich, not just him. Like Obama said, no man left behind. He and Kiki had worked out how it was going to go down as far as how they were going to ensure that PJ, TK, and Reggie ate. With the right plug, the sky was the limit.

"Damn! What, you closed the restaurant for the day?" Taz asked when he pulled into the parking lot and saw it was empty except for a few cars.

"Yeah, because my daddy don't really like being around a bunch of people."

They got out and Isabella grabbed his hand as they walked inside. There were about fifteen Mexicans roaming about. When they entered, all eyes turned to them. Isabella started speaking Spanish, asking them where her dad was. Since meeting Isabella, he had been teaching himself Spanish so he could understand it. He just couldn't speak it too well. Isabella had yet to find this out. She grabbed his hand and pulled Taz toward a table where a man he assumed to be her father was sitting. Before they got to the table, her brother and another Mexican dude stepped in their way.

"Juan!" She jumped in her brother's arms while Taz took in the other dude.

He could tell by the way he was looking and standing that he thought he was a bad ass. Taz made a mental note to avoid him.

"You can't speak, Pablo?" Isabella asked the bad ass.

He started speaking rapid Spanish, He asked her what she was doing dating a monkey. Taz wanted to get mad, but that would've exposed his hand, so he remained calm, as if he was oblivious to the disrespect.

"Fuck you, pussy! Move!" she said, grabbing Taz's hand and moving towards her Daddy's table. "Daddy, this is my boyfriend Taz. Taz, this is my dad Hector."

Pablo snorted behind him.

"It's a pleasure to meet you." Taz extended his hand.

"Hope I can say the same thing after this meeting." He shook Taz's hand and motioned for them to sit down.

"Daddy, he - "

Hector put his hand up, cutting her off. "Taz, my daughter can be a little overzealous at times. I already know she was about to rain praise on you. The main reason I even agreed to this meeting was because Isabella has never tried to introduce any of her friends before. But I did some digging and I found out that my baby girl is dating a gangster."

"Daddy, he's not - "

"Isabella!" Her father cut her off again, causing her to

poke her lips out and pout, which made Taz laugh.

Taz grabbed her hand under the table to soothe her.

"Now Taz, I know who you are, whether or not my daughter does or not. I'm not saying I have too much of a problem with y'all's relationship because she's a grown woman and I know for a fact she can handle herself. My question to you is, what do you want? This meeting was most likely your idea, since I know my daughter, and as I've told you, I did my research. So what's your angle?"

Taz looked across the table at the head of the Mexican Cartel, the most feared cartel in the world, and smiled. He respected his G, but he didn't fear him, so he was going to carry him the same way he did anyone else. He wasn't doing any ass kissing. He looked over at Isabella, not knowing how she was going to read, but he knew she'd be okay.

"I need a plug," he told him, maintaining eye contact.

Isabella snatched her hand out of his and crossed her arms across her chest. Gone was the pout. It was replaced by a scowl directed his way.

"I figured as much, but to my understanding, you are done with the streets," Hector informed him letting him know he had really did his homework.

"That's true to a certain extent, but I'm trying to ensure that my team will have that option after a good run."

"I don't usually take on new clientele, but your pedigree is what's making me even consider this. But I'm going to leave it to Isabella whether or not we do business or not." He grinned.

Taz looked over to Isabella, and she still had a scowl on her face. But he knew she would do whatever he wanted to. Since they had become an official couple, she had put all her trust in him. Anything Taz wanted to do, she wanted to do. She was the model of perfection when it came to the way Taz wanted his wife to be. They rarely, if ever argued, and she knew his likes and dislikes. So he knew since he asked for the plug she might be upset, but she was going to stand behind him.

"So what's your answer?" Hector asked Isabella.

"Yeah," she said immediately.

"That's that. You'll be going through my son Juan. Being that you and my daughter are an item, I'm going to give you a good price. But know this: that is my baby girl, and the way you treat her is the way I'm going to treat you. If you hurt her, you're guaranteeing yourself an early exit from this world."

Taz tensed up at the threat. Isabella reached over and started rubbing the back of his hand to calm his nerves because she knew how he felt about threats.

"I'm also expecting full loyalty from you. My enemies are yours and yours are mines. I'm aware that the issue you had with the Zoe Pound Mafia is taken care of, but don't underestimate that you had the upper hand on him in the last meeting. Zion has a pride issue and a little man complex," Hector informed him, making Taz wonder how in the hell he knew all that he did. "Don't worry yourself trying to figure out how I know what I know. My reach is endless. I have something in the making for Zion. He's a nonfactor."

Taz ignored Hector's last comment.

"Okay, enough business talk. Let's enjoy our meal," he said, and the waiters brought out all kinds of dishes.

There was everything from steak enchiladas to shrimp tacos. While they ate, Isabella and her father carried on a conversation in Spanish. Taz's ears perked up when he asked her if she was serious about him or if he was just someone she was playing with. Isabella told him she was in love with him and that they were planning a future together. After that, their conversation turned back to being boring.

Taz casually checked Hector out. He was short, maybe 5'8", with a low cut. There was nothing special about him, but reading up on him, Taz learned that he was a billionaire. He was featured in the Forbes top 100. He had quite a few businesses, but his bread and butter came from his import/export business. Taz didn't so much care about the businessman. He wanted to know about the cartel leader. Hector wasn't the only one that did his homework.

Doing his research, Taz learned that Hector started out as a foot soldier but worked his way up the ladder. Most climbed it using smarts and loyalty. He reached boss status at twenty years old. But instead of doing what the bosses before him had done and become the face, he played the background, all while he was using his resources to network for his vision. Once he had enough legal money, he started his import/ export business and never looked back. Nowadays, he let his son Juan do most of the work in regards to the cartel. Juan took after his father. He used his brain. He left the dirty work to one of his childhood friends that he was brought up with. They called him the Grim Reaper. He was said to be the modern day boogey man.

"It's about that time." Hector stood up. "It was a pleasure to meet you, Taz. My son already knows to take care of you and to give you whatever is it you want. I have a plane to catch. And Taz?" He looked him in the eye. "Take care of my baby." With that he left, taking everyone with him except Juan, Pablo, and four other dudes.

"Taz, this is my number. All you have to do is let me know what you want and how many, and we'll meet here to handle our business." Juan got right to it.

"A'ight, bet."

They shook hands and he left, leaving the restaurant empty except for Taz and Isabella.

Isabella let the staff leave and came back to the table and started amping on Taz.

"You're a piece of shit! You used me to get a connect! I should've known you weren't shit! You probably knew who my dad was the whole time. Look, I'ma let y'all build a relationship, then tell my dad we not working. That way he'll keep dealing with you, because I'm not," Isabella stated as tears began falling from her eyes.

Seeing her cry was doing something to his insides. He walked over to her and tried to hug her, but she pushed him away.

"Don't fucking touch me!"

"Calm the fuck down!" Taz yanked her up and sat her on a table with him in between her legs. "You don't know what the fuck you talking about! I ain't know shit about your fuck-ass daddy until someone else told me! You should've been the one, but I had to find out from somebody else." She calmed down a little bit because she knew he was mad to be talking to her like that. "So you not dealing with me no more, huh?"

Isabella shook her head no.

"If that's really what you want, then it's okay with me."

He tried to slip away from her, but she wrapped her legs around him and grabbed the front of his shirt.

"Let me go, Bella."

"No, you not leaving me." She wrapped her arms around his neck and scooted to the edge of the table so that her pussy was against his zipper. She took his hand and put it between her legs. "You see how wet you make me?"

Taz pulled his hand away and his fingers were dripping with her juices.

"I'm not dealing with you no more, remember?" He stepped away from her.

"Yes, the fuck you are!" She latched back onto him and

stuck her tongue in his mouth.

"You need to tighten the fuck up with that attitude you got," he warned her before trying to eat her on every table in the restaurant like she had said.

Nicholas Lock

Chapter 16

Taz, PJ, TK, Reggie, and Kiki were in Lafayette Village, a middle-class neighborhood in which Taz had rented a house for them to handle their business. Taz had just left from his first meeting with Juan and everything had gone as planned. Other than Pablo mean mugging him, he had no issues. The price he was getting the work for was something straight out of an urban book.

"I told y'all niggas I had y'all, didn't I? Now all y'all got to do is run a checkup. Look, though, I don't want y'all playing the block. Let the little niggas do that. Just sell weight," Taz said.

"Just how much weight are you talking about?" TK asked.

"Okay, this the deal," Kiki took over. "TK and PJ, y'all getting five bricks of raw apiece. Reggie, you getting fifteen pounds of loud."

"Yo, that work ain't been cut, so y'all should be able to at least turn each bird into two, and Reggie, niggas don't got this strand of loud. It's some shit called Cobra Venom, so you can control the market. Listen when I tell you niggas this. This ain't no long-term thing. Get rich and branch off to the legal world. Y'all can't tell me one big time D-boy that's been selling work for a long time that ain't eventually get picked up by them people. Every single kingpin bit the dust! Even El Capo got snatched up, and he was that nigga! Take it for what it's worth. I ain't trying to see none of y'all locked up," Taz told them.

"This is the spot where we gon' do our business at from now on. We expecting y'all to make up, the sky is the limit. It's New Year's Eve, so we gon' bring the new year in right. We going out tonight to celebrate. We about to put the city on notice. This our shit now, and ain't nothing nobody can do

117

about it!" Kiki amped up.

"That's what I'm talking about," PJ said.

Taz sat and watched as Kiki distributed the work. He had done it; he had made a way for his team to eat. They were about to take off, and there was no ceiling. The question that he kept asking himself was, how much money was enough money? His business acquisitions were already turning over a profit and he hadn't even told them his ideas for helping the business grow. If things kept going how they were, he would be able to say he was a millionaire and it would all be legal money. He hadn't begun to factor in the drug money. When he was younger, all he dreamed about was being that nigga, getting to the money and fucking bitches. But now his goals had changed. He wanted to make sure his daughters had a college education. Also, there was a certain lifestyle that he wanted to live, and he planned on living it by all means. He just had to be sure he didn't get caught back up in the glitz and glamour of the street life. He couldn't explain it, but there was just something about the street life that held a certain appeal, it was downright addictive.

"We about to shake this shit up," Reggie said, rubbing his hands together. "It's the takeover!" he screamed out.

"Calm your ass down," TK said in his usual calm demeanor.

"Where we going to party tonight?" PJ asked.

"Club Atlantis," Taz spoke up.

"Well, I got to go buy me a new outfit," PJ said.

"Let's hit the mall in Raleigh. I'm trying to see what that Gucci store talking about," Reggie said.

"Sounds good to me. Y'all coming?" TK asked Taz and Kiki.

Taz shook his head. "I got a few things I got to handle before tonight," he said.

"And I got to go to the salon because I'm about to shit on these hoes tonight," Kiki informed them.

"Well, we gon' catch y'all later," they said and filed out.

"We still doing that Atlanta lick too, nigga. I don't want to hear nothing but okay either," she said when they left.

"Kiki, gotdamn! Ain't no need, we good! All we got to do is sit back and watch the money roll in."

"Taz, don't play with me. We going to the A next week to scope some shit out, so be ready," she said with finality.

Taz just looked at her. He was going to say something else about it, but thought better of it because the look on her face said it all. If he said something else, she was going to blow a head gasket, and Taz didn't feel like dealing with her attitude. Kiki was like a pitbull because once she locked onto something, she had no plans on letting go.

"A'ight with your spoiled ass," he conceded.

"Straight like that." She grinned. "I'm off to get my hair done, see you tonight." She kissed him on the cheek and left.

Taz looked up and left so he could get ready for the night's activities. Taz didn't hold any punches with the outfit he had chosen to wear out tonight. He had on a white Prada polo, some white Prada pants, and pair of white Prada sneakers. He had finally replaced his presidential Rolex with another one. The only difference was that this one wasn't rose gold; it was white gold. Plus he got a customized chain made with a Tasmanian devil encrusted in blue and white diamonds. He had lost his other grill, so he had a new one made. When he opened his mouth, it was like he had a strobe light in his mouth. The diamond studs in his ear had run him ten bands apiece, but they were the size of your thumbnail. Earlier that day he had gone to the African shop and got the tips of all his dreads dyed white.

"Being this fly should be against the law!" Taz said to

himself while checking his image in the mirror. He pulled his dreads out of the bun he had them in and let them fall. When he first came home, his dreads fell just below his chest, but now they were almost to his belly button. He was going to let them swing tonight. This was going to be his first time out with his boys since his first week home. He was going to have a good time. He wasn't trying to deal with drama or bullshit.

"Nigga, where you at?" Kiki asked when he answered his phone.

"At the house why?"

"I'm riding with you, and make sure you drive that new car," she said.

"How you know about that?" He had kept it on the low.

"Don't worry about it. Just come on," she responded and hung up.

Taz thought he was being slick when he got the new Ferrari. Isabella had A-1 credit, so Taz got the car in her name. He wasn't planning on bringing it out just yet, but why not? New year, new beginnings. He was definitely about to turn heads when he hopped out of the white Ferrari with the all-white Prada outfit and the white-tipped dreads. And Reggie had the nerve to call himself the swag king.

Taz grabbed the keys and made his way to the car. The car alone would grab your attention, but what he loved the most was how the engine growled when you cut it on. Every other car he passed on the way to Kiki's house did a double take, and the limo tint kept them from seeing who was driving.

Every time he pulled into Kiki's neighborhood, he shook his head. For all that ghetto shit she was doing, she lived in an upscale neighborhood. Every single house was two stories. It looked similar to the neighborhood that Gutta lived in. He called and told her he was outside.

"Oh shit!" Taz said when she stepped out of the house.

Kiki didn't lie when she said she was going to shit on them hoes tonight. Her hair was ironed and curled, sitting on the top of her butt. But the main attraction was the white Alexander Wang dress she wore. The sides of it were open with zig zag patterns. It stopped just below her ass cheeks. If she bent over, her ass would be out. It was so tight you would've thought she had gotten poured into it. Kiki surprised him by wearing some six inch white Red Bottoms that strapped all the way up her long legs. She actually looked ladylike, he thought - until she opened her mouth. Kiki had a full set of fronts in.

"Take that damn grill out your mouth."

"Boy, boo. You got to let me drive this," she said as she set her Chanel bag down.

"In your dreams."

On the ride to the club, she filled him in on the plan she had concerning the Atlanta move. He only half-listened because he wasn't trying to hear anything about it, to be honest.

"Are you listening to me?" she asked, putting her finger on his nose.

"Yeah, girl, and get your finger out my face."

"What I say then?"

They pulled into the club parking lot, saving Taz from telling her the wrong answer. As expected, everybody stared at the Ferrari as he parked, waiting to see who was going to get out. When they got out, PJ, TK, and Reggie came over and immediately got on Taz's ass.

"You stunting like a fool!" PJ's animated ass said, walking around the car.

"Yeah, boy, you did that," TK commented.

"You said who the Swag King?" Taz asked, brushing a piece of imaginary lint off his shirt.

"Me, nigga! You can't see?" Reggie said.

Taz wasn't gon' front. Reggie was on his shit. He sported a green and black Burberry blazer, some Burberry jeans, and some black Ferragamo boots. All his niggas were fly though. TK rocked a blue Fendi shirt, black Fendi pants, and some black and blue Balenciaga sneakers. PJ kept it laid back with a simple tan Ralph Lauren dress shirt, tan Ralph Lauren jeans, and tan and white Gucci loafers. And they were all jeweled up.

"If y'all done with trying to see who dick bigger, then we can go inside." Kiki stood with her hands on her hips.

"That's me." Reggie spoke up.

"I don't know, I heard my brother was strapped now."

"Did you hear that, or do you know firsthand?" Reggie smiled.

She gave them the finger and walked towards the club, and all four of them watched her ass jiggle. They caught up to her just as a dude said something to her about leaving with him tonight. Before any of them could check him, Kiki had punched him in the mouth.

"That really ain't what you trying to do," TK said as the dude drew his hand back. He looked at all of them, and when his eyes stopped on Taz, his whole demeanor changed.

"Get your people, brah," the dude told Taz, letting them know he didn't want no drama.

"I told your ass I ain't want no drama tonight" Taz said through clenched teeth as he took Kiki by the elbow and led her to the entrance of the club.

"Get off me!" Kiki tried to snatch her arm away, but Taz wasn't letting go.

"Don't play with me, Keasha," he whispered, dragging her to the VIP area.

"No fucking drama tonight!" Taz reiterated once they all got in VIP.

Kiki rolled her eyes as she sat in the corner brooding.

"Now let's enjoy ourselves," TK said.

They all took off in different directions - everybody except Taz. He grabbed a bottle of Peach Ciroc out one of the ice buckets and turned it up. It had been a long time since he'd been able to let his guard down and relax. And that's exactly what he planned on doing. He just had to keep one eye on Kiki and PJ. They were the ones most likely to get into some shit.

Taz walked to the edge of the booth and looked down over the club. He spotted PJ first. He and Reggie were laughing and joking with some hoes. Then he saw TK standing off to the side, whispering to a thick-ass snowbunny. Then he spotted his girl Kiki. She was in the middle of the floor putting on a show. She was dancing by herself, throwing her ass every which way, having a good time.

This was what it was all about. His team was enjoying themselves and he didn't have any worries. It didn't get too much better than that. Life was treating him well at the moment. He looked back at Kiki and saw a nigga try to dance up on her, and she deaded it. This happened four more times before he made his way down to where she was. He got up on her and started dancing. She stopped dancing and turned to see who it was, but when she saw it was Taz, she really turned up. Taz, not being a slouch in the dance department, went toe to toe with her. Then the DJ played the old club banger "The Percolator" and the whole club got lit! Kiki was too much.

Taz bowed out and started making his way back to the VIP section when he spotted her. She was dancing under the lights. She was high yellow with red dreads that hung past her ass and she was built like a brick house. She had the exact same build as Chinkz from the *Straight Stuntin* magazine. He was battling himself whether or not to say something to her. He thought of his baby Isabella, but shorty was too bad not to say something. She watched him as he walked up to her.

"How you doing, sexy?"

"Fine." She smiled, showing off a set of pearly whites.

"Come chill with me." He grabbed her hand and led her up the steps to the VIP section.

When she asked Taz his name, only then did he realize she had an accent like she was from the islands.

"Taz. And where you from and what's your name?"

"Barbados, and Quanesha, but everybody calls me Nesha. I came over here to go to Fayetteville State University." She referred to the historic black college.

Everybody came back to VIP as she asked him to dance with her. He could tell by their looks they approved. Even Kiki gave her a second look.

Nesha pulled him to the edge of the booth and put all that ass in his lap. Taz was locked in grinding on her when something told him to look up. He looked up from Nesha's ass to look out over the club, only to lock eyes with the last person he expected to see: Isabella.

Chapter 17

Taz backed up off Nesha and took off in Isabella's direction. Before he could get to her, Mary stepped in his path. He tried to move around her, but she moved with him.

"Hold up real quick." He slid around her, trying to spot Isabella, but he didn't see her anymore.

He asked one of the bouncers if they had seen a short Mexican chick, and he pointed towards the door. Taz shot out the door just as Isabella was getting in her car.

"Isabella!" Taz yelled.

She looked at him, but didn't respond. He walked up to her door and tried to open it, but she had locked it.

"Stop playing with me, Bella."

She cracked the window. "I'm good. Go back in there with your whore."

"That's not my whore! I don't even know her, we was just dancing. Why you so fucking insecure? Come on in here and chill with me, bae."

She squinted her eyes at him. "No, but you can come to my house and we can chill there." She raised her brow as if daring him to say no.

"A'ight, man, damn!"

"I'll be there when you get there." She pulled off.

When Taz walked back in the club, Mary was standing there waiting on him.

"You chasing behind hoes now?"

"You don't know what you talking about, Mary."

"So what, you just fuck me and that's it, huh? I mean, I pretty much knew we wasn't going to be a couple, but damn, you could at least call a bitch."

Taz smiled at the way she kept it gutter. "I been mad busy, Mary. I be ripping and running. But you got my word, I'm going to pull up on you in the next few days."

"I'm going to get some of this." She grabbed his wood.

"We might be able to work that out. But let me go, girl." He turned to walk away and she grabbed his hand.

"Keishana said to call her. I don't know what kind of cloak and dagger shit y'all got going on. It's none of my business. But don't have her in no shit, Taz," she warned.

"Got you." He walked off.

Before he could get to the VIP section, he ran into Nesha.

"That must have been your girl you ran after." She smirked.

"Hell yeah," he admitted.

"I ain't tripping. I figured your cute ass had a girl. But do that mean we can't be friends?" she asked.

"Nah, put my number in your phone."

They exchanged numbers. Taz went and told Kiki and them that he was going to catch up with them later. They gave him hell about being pussy whipped. He made sure Kiki had a way home and left, hoping he didn't hear about them doing no bullshit in the morning.

Taz pulled up to Isabella's house at 11:30. He walked in and the house was pitch black. As he got closer to the back, he could hear R. Kelly playing.

When he got to the bedroom, Isabella was lying in the middle of the bed in a pink teddy with the nipples and crotch area open. He thought she was awake, but as he stepped in the room, he saw she was asleep. The only word that came to mind was "angel" as he watched her sleep. He stripped down to his boxers and climbed between his baby's legs. Taz sucked her clit into his mouth, causing her eyes to fly open and her to cry out. He ran his tongue down from her love button all the way down to her ass, making her grab two handfuls of his dreads.

"Oh fuck, papi! You nastyyyy!" She moaned as he ran his tongue around her ass.

"Te amor, papi!" she screamed as she climaxed, coating Taz's face in her juices.

"I love you too, ma, take this off" Taz pulled at the teddy and she just looked at him through half-closed eyes. Her orgasm had her drunk.

"At least help me."

She raised her ass a little bit and he slid her teddy off.

He didn't feel like undoing all the clasps, so he just pushed her bra up over her breasts. He sucked one of her nipples in his mouth and slid between her legs. Taz slipped inside Isabella and began to give her slow steady strokes.

"Baby," she whispered, running her hands through her hair.

"Oh, you can talk now?"

"Shut up," she said meekly.

She pulled his face to hers and stuck her tongue in his mouth as he began to speed his strokes up. Isabella tried to run, but he pinned her down and tried to knock her walls down.

"I'm about to cum, papi!" she yelled and he stopped.

"Nah, you can't nut until I say so." He pulled out and flipped her over so that she was on her stomach.

He put a pillow under her so her ass was tooted up. He pushed her ass up with both hands and aimed his dick between her legs. When he entered her, Isabella clenched the sheets, moaning into a pillow.

"Fuck that! I want to hear that shit!" He grabbed a handful of her hair and yanked back, then started to pound her.

"Taz! Taz! Taaaz! You gon' make me cum!" she yelled.

Taz wouldn't let up. He was trying to knock the bottom

out. He started pulling all the way out and slamming back into her.

"Take this dick, Bella."

After five minutes of this, she screamed that she was cumming. He let her hair go and started giving her short, fast strokes. He filled her with his kids at exactly 11:59. He fell on top of her, out of breath.

"Happy New Year, baby," he said as the clock hit twelve.

They fell asleep just as they were.

Chapter 18

The new year was turning out to be quite lucrative. TK and them had moved up, so much so that they were talking about branching out to another city, and Kiki was pushing for the city to be Atlanta. Plus his business investments were doing numbers. He'd already made his money back so now everything was straight profit. He had a meeting later on with Olivia and Victoria to discuss some ideas on the business. He had gotten Kiki to put off going to the A for a couple weeks, but it looked like he was just going to go ahead and get it over with. In the meantime, he had to call Keishana. He Facetimed her.

"What up, boo?"

"You. Where your clothes at?"

"Nigga, I got clothes on."

"Bra and panties ain't clothes, but anyway, Mary said you wanted me to call you.

"I handled that for you."

"Oh shit! I had forgot about that shit, what I owe you?"

"Don't try to play me, bae. You took care of SK for me, so it was only right that I return the favor. Besides, it was a win/win for me. I hadn't had no real dick in a real long time. I just wish you would've told me he was freaky like that. He called his son over and they ran a train on me," she said not, giving a fuck. Keishana was a dog!

"Wait a minute, his son? What he say his name was?" Taz hoped she wasn't about to say who he thought she was.

"Gutta, why?" she asked, clueless.

Zion had shifted him. He hadn't told anybody his plan, not even Keasha. He had sent Keishana to Miami to seduce the nigga and fuck him without a rubber. Not only did she fuck him, but she got Gutta too. Now they were both dying slow.

Fuck them!

"A'ight, baby girl, you can come on back to the city."

"A'ight."

"Hold up. Before you go back to doing what you doing, let me see it."

"Taz," she whined.

"Shit, I can't fuck you, so what's the harm in it?"

She set her phone up against something and scooted back so he could see her body. She pulled her panties off, revealing the fattest pussy he'd ever seen in his life. He didn't know what she was doing, but she was really taking care of herself because her body was on point.

"Let me see it," she countered.

Taz pulled his dick out and they fucked each other the only way that they were ever going to be able to.

***

"How you doing, Mr. Walker?" Victoria asked as he walked into their office.

Since their deal, Victoria had been on board with him being a part of the business. After a few sit downs with her, he realized she was smart as hell and real business savvy. It probably helped that she had a degree from Harvard. He'd gotten to know her and Olivia well over the last few months, so much so that Victoria had invited him to have dinner with her and her family, which consisted of her husband and her two daughters. Her girls were the same age as his. She led him to the conference room, where Olivia was setting up a PowerPoint presentation.

"What's good, Livy?" he asked.

"Not much, ready to get out of here," she admitted.

Olivia and Taz were on a more personal level. With her being closer to his age at thirty-one, they had more in common. Still, at forty, Victoria was hip to certain things.

"Well, let's get this over with so you can go," he said.

He listened as both of them gave him a rundown on what was going on with the business. They told him where they were making a profit and where things were going kind of slow. After they got done with their presentations, they asked him if he had any ideas.

"Actually I do. I've given this a lot of thought. What do you say about installing a delivery service?"

"I've never given it any thought," Olivia stated.

"Now that you say it, it might actually be a good idea," Victoria said.

"Doing this will bring our bottom line up. I can almost guarantee it," said Taz.

"I'm going to do some research on it and get back to you," Victoria told him.

"Oh, and my girls are having a sleepover this weekend, and I expect to see D'Azia and Neveah there."

"I got you." He laughed.

"I think that sums everything up," Olivia said, obviously ready to go.

"I'll check on y'all in a couple of days," he said and walked out.

He called Kiki when he got outside.

"What you want, nigga?" she answered.

"What the hell you doing?"

"Making myself some Theraflu. I don't feel good."

"I'm about to come through." He hung up.

On the way to Keasha's house, he stopped at Wal-Mart and picked up a few cans of Campbell's chicken noodle soup. When he brought her to Fayetteville back in the day, he was all she had. Whenever she would get sick, he would make her eat some Campbell's and they'd watch movies as he nursed her up. She opened the door and he pulled up.

"I know that ain't no chicken noodle soup." She eyed the bag. "Why you always think that's the cure-all for everything?" She let him into the house.

"Anyway, I didn't know you liked Minnie Mouse." Taz looked her over in her Minnie Mouse pajama set.

She rolled her eyes. Taz went in the kitchen and put on a pot of soup. He came back out in the living room as she was crawling under a comforter.

"What's wrong, Keasha?" He sat down on the couch beside her.

"My head, throat, eyes, hell, everything hurts," she told him.

"I told your ass about going out half-ass dressed, but your ass hardheaded."

"Leave me alone," she groaned, pulling the covers over her head.

Taz got up to check on the soup. He made her a bowl and sat back down beside her.

"Sit up, woman!"

"Ughh." She sat up and he began feeding her the soup. He made her eat the whole bowl, then he got up and put the movie *Baby Boy* on. He took his shoes off and got comfortable on the couch. Five minutes into the movie, Kiki crawled into his lap and curled up.

"You too big for this, girl."

She didn't respond. She put her head in the crook of his neck and got comfortable. Taz wrapped his arms around her and left her alone. Before he knew it, he could hear her snoring softly. Most people thought Kiki was just this hardcore gangster chick, but really she was soft as hell. What people

132

failed to realize was that Keasha was still a woman. She wanted to be loved and cared for just like the next woman. Plus she was still dealing with the demons from her past. She was still scarred from her childhood. It was going to take a special kind of dude to deal with her and her past, and that's mainly the reason Taz ran off the dudes that tried to holler. Most of them just wanted some ass. They wasn't looking for a long-term relationship. He had a bonafide soft spot for her.

When he first brought her back, she was more like his daughter than anything else. He took care of her every need, and she was even sleeping in the bed with him. His boys tried to holler at her, but Taz nipped that in the bud. She wasn't supposed to turn out the way she did. Her robbing and shooting was never his intention. He wanted her to go to school. But after she stabbed a girl at school, that was the end of that. Taz took her under his wing and gave her the game and it's been on ever since. He had already made up his mind that when they went to ATL, he was going to reach out and see what he could find out about her parents. They should be out of prison now. That way his girl could get some closure on her past.

In the meantime, he was going to nurse and baby her up. He carried her to her bed, climbed in with her, and they both went to sleep.

Chapter 19

"Do y'all have y'all pajamas in the bag?" Taz asked his girls. He was getting ready to drop them off at Victoria's.

"Yes," they said in unison.

"Don't let me get no phone call about y'all acting up." He looked in the rearview mirror.

He was more so talking to Neveah. She was a real problem child. She had developed a mean streak. The school stayed calling because she had a problem keeping her hands to herself. And it didn't matter whether it was a boy or a girl. D'Azia was his little angel. She didn't get in trouble and she was super smart. They were talking about skipping her up a grade.

They pulled up to Victoria's house just as some kids were getting dropped off. He got out and walked them to the door. His mood darkened when Victoria opened the door.

"Hey girls! Come on in. All the girls are upstairs in Elizabeth's room," she said.

His girls took off upstairs and Victoria tried to follow them, but Taz grabbed her hand.

"What happened to your face?" Her face was black and blue on the left side.

"Me being clumsy. I ran into the kitchen cabinet," she said looking at the ground.

Taz knew she was lying, but he was going to let it go. The bruise was the shape of a fist. He hated dudes that put their hands on women! Regardless of the situation, he felt you should never put your hands on a female. They weren't built to withstand that kind of punishment. He hoped a nigga didn't ever put their hands on one of his daughters, because if someone did that, he was going back to prison.

"You got to be more careful. Call me if they give you any

trouble," he said, turning to leave.

"Daddy, look!" Neveah and D'Azia ran towards him with snakes in their hands. "Elizabeth and Tanya have pet snakes!" they said as a group of girls came down the stairs.

"You watching all these kids?" There were fifteen nine and ten year olds in all. A migraine waiting to happen.

"Olivia was supposed to help, but she stood me up and my husband got called out of town on business."

"I got a few hours of free time," he offered, even though it was against his better judgement.

"Great! You can help me with the food."

Victoria had made a bunch of chicken fingers and French fries. He helped her make the kids' plates. All the while there was utter chaos around him. There were kids running back and forth, kids jumping on couches, kids chasing a dog around, and Victoria acted as if this was normal. His nerves were going to be shot when he left.

"Aye, aye, aye, aye! Go wash y'all hands so y'all can eat," he said.

They got them to sit down long enough to eat, and he and Victoria sat down in the living room. He was tired already.

"We did the research on offering delivery as an option, and we think you might be right. The upside is off the charts. We should have it up and running in the next two months, if things go according to plans," she informed him.

"I kind of figured it would work out."

"We're done, Mom!" Tanya yelled from the kitchen.

She went to clean up the dishes and Taz herded them upstairs, where he made them take showers and change into their pajamas. He ordered the new X-Men movie on the TV and they immediately looked in. When he walked back downstairs into the kitchen, Victoria had her back to him, arguing on her cell phone.

"What the hell, Brad! I've been so good to you! I put up with all your abuse. I got a damn black eye, Brad! Who is she? I see all the signs. The late meetings, the perfume on your clothes. I know you didn't get called out on business because I checked. I know you're with her now, but fuck you, Brad! You heard me! Fuck you! She can have you and your little cock!" She hung up and broke down crying.

Taz was going to grab his keys and leave because she needed some time alone. He snuck into the living room, got his keys, and was trying to creep back out when she turned around.

"D'angelo, why is it the better you treat someone, the worse they treat you?"

"Victoria, I can't answer that."

"I've been with this man for twenty-two years! He's the only man I've ever known and loved. I put my all into this marriage, and I get shit in return," she cried.

Sometimes the best words are the ones not spoken, so instead of responding, he wrapped her in a hug and she cried harder.

"Let it out, ma."

They sat down on the couch with Victoria soaking his shirt in her tears. He felt sorry for making her cry harder.

"You going to be alright?" He continued to hold her.

"Keep me company for a little while." She looked at him, eyes red and puffy from all the crying she was doing.

"I got you."

They sat there in silence watching TV and before he knew, it he had dozed off. When he woke up, it was 2:30 in the morning. Victoria had laid down with her head in his lap and gone to sleep. He was trying to figure out how to get up without waking her up. As he tried to slide from up under her, she repositioned herself and placed her hand under her head, which just so happened to be right on top of his dick. The friction of her hand along with his jogging pants caused his little man to rock up. Taz's eyes got big. He definitely had to get up now. He tried to slide away again, only for her hand to close around his dick through his jogging pants and her eyes flew open.

"Oh my gosh! D'angelo, I'm sorry!" she said upon realizing she had a handful of his dick.

"You straight," he said as she sat up and wiped her eyes.

"Wait a minute, what are you doing with an erection?" She squinted at him.

Taz laughed at how proper she talked. "I just woke up."

"Oh," she said, staring at his lap. "Um, don't take this the wrong way, but you are big." She pointed at his print.

The conversation was starting to get risqué and he wasn't trying to have his business dealings messed up, so he got up and started looking for his keys.

"I'm sorry if I made you uncomfortable." She smirked.

"Yeah, right, I'm just trying to find my keys," Taz said passively, trying to avoid the conversation

"You know, I've never been with anyone but my husband sexually." She got bolder. "And from the looks of it, you're bigger than him by at least six inches." She continued to stare at this dick print.

Taz was trying to get the hell away from her because she was starting to get carried away. She was going from a heartbroken spouse to a horny cougar.

"You looking for these?" She held up his keys

"Toss them here."

"Come get them." She put them in her bra.

Taz was starting to lose his patience with her. He was trying to be nice and not hurt her feelings. If she wasn't a snowbunny, he'd fuck her.

"Give me my damn keys, Victoria." He walked up on her.

"No," she said with a mischievous gleam in her eyes.

He was about to say the hell with their business dealings and hurt her feelings. Fuck it! He reached for her bra to get his keys and she moved to the other side of the couch.

"Yo, stop playing with me." He gritted his teeth. It was amazing how she went from crying to playing.

"What you gonna do if I don't? You not tough. I see through that tough guy act. You really a pussy!" she teased.

Before she knew it, he grabbed a handful of her hair and snatched her shirt, ripping both her shirt and bra, causing her breasts to spill out, revealing a set of D-cups with hard nipples.

"Oh, D'angelo! How'd you know I like it rough?"

This bitch crazy! he thought to himself. When he went to grab his keys, she grabbed his dick through his jogging pants.

"Let me the fuck go!" This was the closest he'd ever come to hitting a woman.

"D'angelo, my husband's cheating on me. I haven't been fucked in six months, nor have I ever been fucked by a black dude. Look how wet I am."

Taz didn't know she did it, but she had come out of her pants and panties. She dipped her hand between her legs, and when she pulled them away, her hand looked like it had been under a water faucet. She had him. He pulled his dick out and stuffed it in her mouth. He grabbed her hair and started to fuck her mouth like he was in some pussy.

"Suck that dick!"

Taz pushed his dick all the way in her mouth and down her throat, trying to make her gag, but she took him all the way down her throat. And licked his balls! She was a fool! She grabbed his dick and ran her tongue around the head and down the sides. Victoria sucked his balls in her mouth while jacking his dick.

"Damn, girl." This was the best top he'd ever gotten.

"Mmm," she moaned, sticking her tongue in the tip of his dick.

He grabbed one of her nipples and twisted it in his fingers.

"Do it harder," she moaned, slapping his dick on her tongue. Taz twisted harder and she moaned louder. *This bitch crazy*, he thought to himself again.

"I'm about to nut, Victoria." He stood up on his tip toes.

"Put it on my face." She started to jack him off with one hand and massaged his balls with the other.

As Taz began to nut, Victoria aimed his dick at her face, painting her face with his kids. Taz fell back on the couch as Victoria rubbed his semen all over her face and licked her fingers.

"You a freak bitch."

"I don't know what's gotten into me, but I know what's about to be in me." She climbed onto hip lap.

"Whoa, whoa! I ain't got no condom."

"I'm clean. Are you?"

"Hell yeah."

She rested one hand on Taz's shoulder and tried to guide him in with the other. She was so wet, she was dripping her juices all over Taz's dick. She got the head in and tried to ease down, but couldn't.

"Your cocks too big." She continued trying to lower herself on him. "I told you that you were way bigger than Brad."

"Watch out." Taz got up and laid her on the floor. He rubbed his head between her legs, getting it wet before he tried to slide inside her. He had to work his way in, and when he got halfway in, Victoria started moaning.

"Oh gosh! You're splitting me open!"

Taz wanted to laugh, but the way her pussy was squeezing

his dick, he had to focus on not busting.

"Fuck! Fuck! Fuck!" she moaned as Taz worked his way all the way in. Once he got all the way in, he gave her enough time to adjust and then pinned her legs up by her ears and started dragging her.

"Oh! Fuck this cunt with your big black cock!" she moaned as he pounded away at her insides. "Choke me," she said, making Taz stop in mid-stroke.

"Huh?" he thought he was tripping.

"Choke me," she said again, taking one of his hands and placing it around her neck.

Fuck it. Taz choked her while pumping away.

"Damn, this pussy tight." He clenched his teeth.

"I'm cumming! I'm cumming!" she said as her body locked up.

Taz let her catch her breath then flipped her over. He wanted to get behind her wide ass. Her butt wasn't fat, but it was wide as hell. He pushed her face all the way down in the carpet and slid in more easily this time.

"Ughh!" She moaned.

He wasted no time. He started stroking her long and hard. "No you not! Take this dick, bitch! This what you wanted," he told her as she started trying to ease away from the pounding he was giving her.

"Wait, wait, wait." she stopped him.

"What's up?" he asked.

"I want to try something." She leaned up so that his dick came out of her, then she reached her hand back between her legs and grabbed his dick. She lifted it up and put it to her asshole. Taz tried to push in, but she hollered.

"No! No! Let me do it first."

She eased back onto his dick, slipping it inside her little by little. Taz thought her pussy was tight, but her ass was even tighter! Once he was halfway in, he took over. He started to slow stroke and she lost it.

"Oh, D'angelo! Fuck my ass!" she moaned, rocking back into him.

Taz started to jackhammer her ass. He wasn't showing any more mercy. Between her moans and him grunting, he didn't know how the kids hadn't woke up. He felt his nut coming, so he sped up more and sprayed his kids in her ass.

She wasn't his bitch, so he wasn't about to lay up with her. He went and cleaned up and when he came back out, she was nowhere to be seen. But he did see she had set his keys on top of his clothes.

Taz drove home and didn't even make it in the house. Victoria had worn him out. He went to sleep in the car.

Chapter 20

"Hey, Juan." Isabella greeted her brother as he and Pablo entered the office in the back of Micasita's

"Que pasó, hermana? What up, Taz?"

"I can't call it," Taz said.

"You need to show some respect. We come in here, and you sitting in his lap. You need to get up and go do some work," Pablo stated in heavy accent.

Before Taz could check him, Isabella did, and her words gave Taz some insight as to why Pablo was always looking at him sideways.

"I know what your problem is, Pablo," she started in. "You just mad because I'm not sitting in your lap. Maybe if you'd been man enough to stand up to my father, you'd still have me. That and the fact that you're lacking in a certain department." She held up her pinky finger, letting everyone know what department that was.

He made a move as if to come where they were sitting, and Juan put his hand on his shoulder and told him to chill.

"Yeah, come get your issue," Taz dared.

Pablo smiled at Taz "If you knew who I was, you'd shut your mouth. You don't know death when you see it? Have you ever met the Grim Reaper?"

Oh shit! So he was the one they referred to as the Grim Reaper.

"If you knew who I was, you'd know the Grim Reaper shit only holds weight in Mexico. You in my city!" Taz started getting hyped. He moved Isabella off his lap and stood up.

As soon as he stood up, Pablo produced a knife, rushed Taz, and had it at his neck before he could react, cementing the fact that he was a certified problem. Juan tried to separate them, but Pablo wasn't having it.

"I could kill you right now, you worthless piece of shit." Pablo pushed the blade deeper into Taz's neck, drawing blood.

"And where would your family live? Mine would kill them all." Taz looked him in the eyes, letting him know he went just as hard.

Click! Clack! Isabella put her pistol to the back of his head. "Let him go now!"

"Or what? You going to shoot me, Isabella?"

POW! She shot him in the foot, causing Pablo to let go of Taz. Taz rushed him and hit him in the mouth, causing him to lose the knife. They started going toe to toe, and even with the bullet wound, he was giving Taz a run for his money.

Then the door busted in and a whole crew of Mexican Mafia ran in with their guns drawn. They took in the scene, Juan just watching the fight, Isabella with her gun in her hand, and Taz and Pablo fighting. They started to move towards the fight.

"No!" Isabella yelled and they stopped. Isabella had just as much say so as Juan, if not more, because it was no secret that she was her father's favorite. So they obeyed her commands too. She rarely exercised her power.

"Let them get it out their system," Juan said, in awe of the fight.

Taz and Pablo were still going toe to toe, neither one wanting to give the other an inch. The crew couldn't believe it. They had never seen anybody go for more than a few seconds against Pablo. They were both tired and out of breath, but neither was going to stop. Taz used the bullet wound in Pablo's foot to his advantage. He stepped on Pablo's foot and connected with an upper cut that sent him to the ground.

"That's enough." Juan stepped in. "Take him to the Doc's house." As they led Pablo out, he shot Taz a look that said the issue was far from being settled.

Isabella came over and started trying to doctor his face. He had a busted lip and some bruises on his face.

"I hope y'all are done acting like kids. Father is going to be mad you shot Pablo," Juan said.

"He started it. He should be glad I ain't kill him."

"Taz, you gon' have to ignore him. He's in love with my sister, and now that you just got the best of him in front of her and the crew, it isn't going to sit well with him. He's going to try you again," Juan told him.

"Next time, it's not going to be fists I'm throwing," he warned.

Juan shook his head. They conducted their business and Juan told Taz that his dad said if he kept increasing his orders the way he was doing, then he was going to drop the price and give him a bonus.

"Why you ain't tell me you used to date Pablo?"

"It was inconsequential. I'm yours now."

"You're right," he said, pulling her back onto his lap and lifting her dress up so he could mark his territory.

***

"Oh shit, nigga! What happened to your face?" Reggie asked.

"You should see the other dude," said Taz.

"Has Kiki seen that?" TK asked, knowing how overprotective she was.

"Have I seen what?" She walked into the room "What. The. Fuck. Happened. To. Your. Face?"

"My shit ain't that bad, y'all overreacting," Taz said.

"They really is. Your lip just busted and your eye a little black, other than that, you still ugly as ever," PJ said.

They were all at the house in Lafayette Village. Kiki knew

145

Taz was going to keep putting the trip to Atlanta off, so she went and convinced everyone that they should all go to the "A" and check out what the potential looked like as far as expanding. Being the suckers they were when it came to Kiki, they agreed. It seemed like Taz was the only one that could tell her no, so they were getting ready to hit the peach state.

"We got to hit Magic City," Reggie said.

"Magic City? Nah, nigga, Diamonds of Atlanta," PJ said.

"Magic City throwing a party and it's supposed to be lit," Keasha said.

Taz knew the real reason she wanted to go to the party, and it had nothing to do with it being lit.

"Come on, before we miss our flight," Taz said.

Taz had booked them in first class, and he made sure to tell them to behave beforehand. He knew when they all got together his niggas cut up. They had no filter. And sure enough, as soon as they got seated, they started acting like fools.

"Excuse me, but can I get a real drink?" Reggie asked the flight attendant, showing her the palm size liquor bottle.

"And I need some directions," PJ said.

"Where?" she said.

"To the Mile High Club," PJ stated, causing her to turn bright red.

"You going to have to excuse my friend. He don't get out much" Taz said.

She nodded as if she understood and went to fix Reggie his drink.

Taz looked over at Kiki, and she was looking out the window. The way they were seated, he and Kiki were on the side. Kiki had the window seat and Reggie, PJ, and TK were to the left of them in the middle seats. Reggie had the aisle and PJ was in the middle of them.

"Are you familiar with Atlanta?" Reggie asked a different flight attendant. She was a super pretty dark-skinned chick.

"Yeah, why?"

"This is my first time going and I'd love for you to show me around."

"I might be able to work that out." She smiled, obviously liking what she saw.

"Hey Reggie, don't forget to take your medicine, we don't need you having an outbreak," Kiki said and the flight attendant took off.

Taz, PJ, and TK cracked up laughing.

"Act like y'all been somewhere before," Kiki said sternly and went back to looking out the window.

Something wasn't right. PJ and TK went to getting on Reggie's case while Taz turned Kiki's way.

"What's wrong, Keasha?"

"Nothing."

"Keep it up," he warned.

"I'm just thinking, do you mind?" she snapped.

Taz looked at her like she was crazy, but said nothing. He was going to let her have that one. He figured she was on her period. But Taz, knowing Kiki, knew it was something a little more than that. He leaned his seat back and was about to try and get some sleep when Kiki turned his way and mushed him in the side of the head. He looked at her, still not saying nothing.

"I want to meet my parents. I want to find out why they left me with that pedophile. Do I have any siblings, some grandparents? The last time I seen my mom, I was seven. Then she got locked up and I went and stayed with my aunt and sick uncle. How come they haven't tried finding me? I got so many questions that need answering," she vented.

"Check this. When this is over, we going to put everything

we got into finding out where they are, but in the meantime, I need you focused. We going to scope this team out so we can hit them and be done with it."

"Okay," she said and then leaned back and closed her eyes.

Taz did the same thing and before he knew it, he had dozed off.

They touched down at Atlanta's Hartsfield Jackson airport a few hours later. They had their rentals waiting outside, so as soon as they got their bags, they headed out. Taz had rented them three Challengers. He knew if he let Kiki rent the cars, everybody would've had Maserati's, and Taz was trying to keep a low profile. PJ got in with TK, Reggie got one by himself, and Kiki rode with Taz. They had rooms at the Hilton in downtown Atlanta. Their rooms were all side by side with Kiki's right beside Taz's. After getting their rooms together TK, Reggie, PJ, and Kiki went to hit the mall, but Taz chose to stay at the hotel and relax.

He was trying to sneak a nap in when his phone rang. It was Victoria. Taz hadn't spoke to her since their sexcapade.

"Hello"

"Hi, D'angelo."

"What's good, Victoria?"

"I'm calling to tell you that we're in the process of setting up the delivery service. We're way ahead of schedule. If we keep this pace, we'll be ready by next month," she said excitedly.

"Sounds good to me."

"One more thing. About the other night - "

"You good, Victoria, you ain't got to explain," Taz cut her off.

"I don't want to mess our business up, but if you say everything's good, then I guess it's good. Can I ask you a question?"

"What's up?"

"Um, was it good?" she whispered shyly.

Taz started laughing. "Yeah, Vicky, it was real good." He thought about how she put him to sleep.

"Thank you. Okay, bye." She hung up.

Taz turned his phone off and went to sleep.

Boom! Boom! Boom!

Taz jumped awake.

Boom! Boom! Boom!

Someone was banging on his door. He went and looked out the peephole only to see it was Kiki.

"What the fuck you banging on my door like that for?" He opened the door.

"I been calling your ass for the last thirty minutes and your phone been off! It's almost time to go." She brushed past him.

"A'ight, girl, damn! What time is it?"

"Eight-thirty."

Taz took a quick shower and when he got out, she was sitting on his bed watching TV.

"Don't you have to go get ready?"

"I been ready."

Taz looked her over. He knew she expected him to say something because the black dress she wore was too short, but he wasn't even in the mood.

"Bye, let me get dressed."

"I'm not in your way," she continued, watching the TV.

"Whatever."

Taz let his towel fall and started lotioning his body.

"I don't see what all these hoes be going crazy about, you not that big."

"Oh, you got me fucked up! First off, it ain't hard, and second off, my stroke game like that."

"Boy, boo!" She laughed.

"You playing. When he stand up, he long as your arm."

"Oh, nigga, I got to see it to believe it." She reached for his dick.

He jumped out her reach. "Don't get fucked up!"

She ran up on him and grabbed ahold of his wood.

"Kiki, you got about two seconds to let me go before I bust your shit."

"That's all I needed anyway." She backed up and looked at his now rock hard dick. "They might be onto something." She walked back to the bed.

Taz ran up and grabbed her and forced her to the bed onto her stomach. "So you want to play, huh?"

"Nigga! You better get the fuck off me!" She tried to wiggle away.

"Nah, you want to play." Taz lifted her dress over her ass and nudged his knee between her legs, forcing them open.

"Taz, I swear to God!"

He walked his hand up her leg until he got to her thong, then he snatched it off.

"Ow, nigga! When I get up, I'm going to fuck. You. Up!" She started thrashing around, trying to get up, and ended up on her back with Taz between her legs. Taz looked between her legs and saw that she was dripping wet.

"Oh, you like that rough shit. Your stanking-ass pussy wet." He got up off her and she sprang.

She tackled him to the floor and somehow got his arms pinned under her knees, which put her pussy in his face.

"Nigga, I should pound your ass out." She slapped him two times.

"Slap me again, Kiki, and that's your ass." He eyed her wet slit.

"Apologize and kiss my kitty cat." She moved up until her pussy was almost to his mouth. He stuck his tongue out and flicked it across her clit, making her jump up. "Oh my God, you - " was all she got out.

Taz put her on the bed and climbed between her legs. He rubbed his dick head up and down her slit and she moaned. They looked in each other's eyes as he placed his dick at her opening. He was about to enter her when somebody knocked on the door, bringing them to their senses. Taz threw on some boxers and Kiki answered the door.

"He getting dressed. We'll meet y'all downstairs," said Kiki.

When she came back to where Taz was at, he had gotten dressed and was sitting on the bed.

"Come here," he said.

She walked over to where he was at and he pulled her onto his lap facing him.

"We almost fucked up, Kiki. I love you. You my little sister. We can't cross that line, even though we might want to. We going to act like this never happened, okay."

"Yeah, and I love you too, Taz." She kissed him on the lips. "Plus if I would've gave you this pussy, you would've been peeking in my window and stalking me and shit," she joked.

"Yeah, right, that stank-ass shit."

They joked all the way to the car as if nothing had happened.

Nicholas Lock

Chapter 21

Magic City was packed. There was barely enough room to walk. They were turning people away because they were at capacity. Kiki showed Taz a picture of OTF's head honcho Marvin and told him to be on the lookout. They were trying to figure out who all was in his crew and find out what kind of position they played. The plan with setting one of the head dudes up had fallen through because the chick didn't fuck with him no more, plus she didn't know who or what the other major players looked like. Everybody had split up, but Taz made sure to keep them in his sights. Taz decided to have a little fun while he was looking for Marvin. As soon as Taz sat on one of the couches against the wall, a thick, pretty Asian chick walked in between his legs. All she wore was stars over her nipples and a lime green G-string.

"You want a lap dance?" she asked, leaning over, putting her hands on his thighs.

Taz nodded his head and she climbed in his lap and started winding her hips. He pulled out a knot of ones and started making it rain on her. When she looked back and saw the size of the knot in his hand she leaned over, put her hands on the floor and started popping her ass one cheek at a time.

"Damn!" he said, running his hand along the thin material of her G-string. She turned around and Taz pulled the stars off her nipples. She lifted one of her legs and put it on his shoulder then the other one so that both of her legs rested on his shoulders. Then she leaned back, put her hands on his knees and arched her back, putting her in the bridge formation. She started to dance like this with her pussy at eye level. Taz pulled one of the strings, untying her G-string. Now her pussy was really in his face. He leaned in and smelled her and was surprised she smelled good. Taz blew on her pussy and her lips peeled back, opening all the way up. She eased back when this happened.

"You going to get me in trouble," she said, righting herself. "My bad."

"It's okay. I'm about to go onstage. You better not go nowhere, because I'm coming back." She sashayed away.

No sooner had she left than PJ, TK, and Reggie walked up.

"We see you, nigga!" PJ said.

"What that pussy smell like?" Reggie asked.

"No, what it taste like?" TK asked.

"You a nasty dog. Remind me not to eat or drink behind this nigga." PJ said.

"Y'all got me twisted! I ain't eat that bread. I did smell it though," he admitted

"Bro, I been asking niggas what the prices is down here and for the most part, we got them beat," TK informed him.

"It wouldn't be nothing to take this shit over. We would have this shit like BMF did," Reggie stated, and Taz could see the dollar signs in his eyes.

"Only thing is this crew called OTF. They got the city sewed up, but they work be so stepped on that niggas say it's hard for them to flip the work," PJ said.

Taz took all their information in. He'd already figured they'd be able to take over. The work they were getting was second to none. His only worry was at what cost. They weren't going to just roll over and give their claim up. Then to top it off, they were out of towners. There were going to be some people that were going to take offense to that prospect by itself, let alone them taking over. He'd have to discuss it with Kiki because what he wasn't willing to pay was any of his people dying. Plus he was getting ready to step away from the game and focus more on his businesses. The next time he met with Pablo he was going to explain this to him but he was going to try and replace himself with TK He was the more stable of the three. If PJ and Reggie didn't cut up so much he would've given them a little more thought. But the stakes were a little too high.

"There go your girl." Reggie pointed.

Taz looked to where he was pointing and saw the Asian chick on the main stage giving it up. She was upside down on the pole, making her ass go. Niggas were going crazy, raining all kinds of money down on her. They locked eyes as she dropped into a handstand and shook her legs, making her ass jiggle.

"That bitch an animal," PJ remarked.

"I don't know, boy, I might would've ate that pussy too," TK joked.

"I see where this is going." Taz stood up.

"Ooohh shit!" Reggie got excited "There go your bitch for real."

Taz looked and Blacc Chyna walked into the club wearing a white body suit. They all knew Taz had a thing for Blacc Chyna. He wasn't leaving without saying something. Isabella be damned, he'd wife Blacc Chyna up no ifs, ands, or buts. Before he could take off in her direction, TK asked, "Why Kiki change?"

"What you mean?" Taz inquired.

"When we left, she had a black dress on, now she got a yellow one on." He pointed.

Sure enough, Kiki was walking past them in a bright yellow dress that looked damn good against her pitch black skin. Taz took off after her because he wanted to know why she had changed too. When he caught up to her, she was standing in the middle of the club swaying back and forth to the music. Taz crept up on her and slapped her on the ass. She turned around and tried to slap him, but he wrapped her up in a hug.

"Why you change? Better yet, where did you go to change at?"

"Nigga, you better get your fucking hands off me unless you want to die tonight."

Hold up. That face was right, but the voice wasn't

"Say that again," he said.

"You heard me, motherfucker!"

"Oh shit!" He let her go and took a few steps back. He had to really look at her and the more he did, he saw something wasn't right. While he was trying to put it together, she slapped the shit out of him. No sooner had she slapped him than she stumbled to the side. All Taz saw was a black blur shoot past him. Kiki landed on her stomach, then Taz saw that the black blur was a chick in a black dress and she was about to stomp Kiki out! Taz ran over and lifted her up before her foot could come down.

"Taz let me down!"

"What the fuck! He put the chick down and she turned around. It was Kiki!

Then he looked to where the chick in the yellow was that he thought was Kiki. She was getting up off the floor, when Taz saw her face he was fucked up. It was Kiki! He looked from Kiki to… Kiki.

"What up, bro?" PJ came over, ready to cut up, then he saw what Taz was seeing. "Oh shit!"

Kiki in the black was staring at Kiki in the yellow. Then OTF's top dog Marvin walked up with an army of niggas and looked at Kiki in the yellow and asked "What's going on, Measha?"

156

"Measha?" Taz repeated

"Oh my God! Keasha!" a woman yelled. And when Taz looked there was another Kiki, only this one was older.

"Ma?" Kiki said hesitantly.

Then the older Kiki ran and wrapped her arms around the real Kiki. Taz just watched as they embraced, Kiki had found her mom.

"Marvin, you better come hug your daughter!"

Oh shit! Shit had just got real. Kiki's parents ran OTF!

Nicholas Lock

Chapter 22

After their emotional reunion, Kiki's mom tried to whisk her away, but Taz was having none of it. He wasn't letting her out of his sights. They didn't have his trust yet. When Kiki saw what was going on she grabbed his hand and introduced them.

"Ma, this is my brother, guardian angel, and my best friend, Taz. Taz, this is my mom, Kiana."

She looked him over the way mothers do, trying to decide if he was worthy of the praise her daughter had bestowed upon him. Taz went to try and shake her hand and she slapped his hand away and hugged him. Her husband eyed him like a hawk. Taz kept his hands above her waist.

"If my baby says you're okay, then you're okay. Marvin, we're leaving and going to the house. Round everybody up. We'll be in the car." She gave the command and tried to pull Kiki away, but Taz had her other hand.

"Kiki going to ride with me and we going to follow y'all," Taz said.

"Honey, I haven't seen my daughter in years. There is no way I'm letting her out my sight," Mrs. Kiana told Taz.

"Guess you're riding with us then," Taz said.

Taz saw a look flash across her face. It was gone just as quick as it appeared, but he caught it. It was the look of malice, one he knew all too well. She obviously wasn't used to being given directives. The more Taz was in her presence, the more he was beginning to think that they had it all wrong. Marvin wasn't the head. It was his wife. She had a commanding aura.

She turned and told her husband, "I'm riding with them."

"Ain't no way in hell," Measha said.

"Yeah, Ma, you don't know them," a short black dude said.

"What I say! And what you mean I don't know them? She came out my pussy, so I think I know her. Besides, she wouldn't let nothing happen to her mother." She focused her grey eyes on Kiki.

Taz let go of Kiki's hand and grabbed her mom's. She looked at him and smirked as he led her out of the club. Reggie, TK, and PJ followed suit. When Taz looked around, he noticed their group had grown to about fifty people. He was slipping. He didn't know they had this many people with them.

When they got to the car, Kiki was going to climb in the back, but her mom said she was getting in the back. Taz helped her and as she bent over to get in the back, she stumbled. Taz steadied her by grabbing her hips and ass. She was too thick not to grab a feel.

"Don't get fucked up!" Kiki gave him a look.

"Watch your mouth, Keasha," her mom warned and Kiki sat back in her seat and poked her lips out.

Taz laughed and pulled out behind the blue Bentley Azure that Marvin had gotten in. Mrs. Kiana leaned up and whispered in his ear "I'm too much for you, little boy" and sat back.

Damn, he thought he was being slick with copping a feel as she was stumbling. He looked in the rearview mirror and saw her looking at him with those piercing grey eyes. He saw where Kiki got it from. He was starting to rethink his decision of letting her sit behind him.

They drove to the outskirts of Atlanta and pulled up to a mansion. Theirs was the only house for almost a quarter mile. The shit was huge. There had to be at least ten bedrooms. They pulled around back and Taz saw an Olympic style in-ground pool. Further in the back it looked like they had a horse barn. Yeah, they were eating. As Kiki helped her mother out, he slipped his fire on his hip.

"Who is these people?" PJ asked.

"Oh shit," TK said when Taz explained to them that they were the OTF crew that ran ATL and that they were Kiki's people.

"Y'all got y'all hammers?" Taz questioned.

"Wouldn't leave home without it." Reggie patted his hip.

They followed everyone in and Taz saw the inside was just as breathtaking as the outside. They came in through the back, which was a giant sunroom with yellow furniture, then they made their way to the main part of the house. It was almost like standing in a museum with the size of it. The living room was huge and was accented by the domed ceilings that had angels drawn on them. The dining room table could seat ten people and the kitchen was something straight out of a DuPont Registry. What Taz liked most was the winding staircase. As he was taking everything in, he was also taking everybody in. He saw Mrs. Kiana trying to lead Kiki away out the side of his eye.

"Whoa, whoa, whoa, where y'all going?" he asked.

"I'm going to talk to my daughter. We have a lot of catching up to do. Everyone here is family. Y'all need to get acquainted anyway.

"Check this. I understand you want to catch up, but I'm not letting Kiki out my sight."

"Who you think you talking to, nigga?" another dark skinned dude asked. "You better recognize where you at and who you talking to." He drew his gun, causing PJ, Reggie, and TK to draw theirs.

They were outgunned and outmanned, and Taz still smiled. "Nah, homeboy, you might not realize who it is your dealing with," Taz said as Kiki slid up on him and put her pistol to the back of his head.

"Everyone put your guns down. That's an order," Mrs. Kiana said and her team complied, cementing what Taz had thought. She was the real boss.

"Keasha, take that gun off your brother now," she demanded, but Kiki looked to Taz, asking him with her eyes what to do. He nodded and she dropped the gun, then Reggie, PJ, and TK did too.

"I don't know who you think you are, boy, but - " her father started to say, but Taz cut him off.

"Who I am is the nigga that saved your daughter from that pedophile you left her with. I'm the one that's been taking care of her while y'all been down here living the good life. I'm the one that'll kill your ass and go to the beach and sip margaritas."

"Let's all just take a breath. We've gotten started on the wrong foot. Let me make some introductions," Mrs. Kiana said. "This is Keasha. She's the daughter we've been looking for, Measha's twin. Keasha, the boy you had your gun on is your little brother Marcus, and the one beside him is your baby brother Kevin. The tall boy with the cornrows is your cousin Jeremy, and the girl beside him is his sister Jaleesa. Everybody else is either security or workers. Now do your part, Keasha."

"Look this is Reggie, PJ, and TK. They're family, they're brothers. And this nigga right here…" She walked over to Taz and put her arm around his waist. "Is my better half. No, he's not my boyfriend. We're more than that. I can't explain it, but know this: if you hurt him, you hurt me. He bleeds, I bleed; he shoots, I shoot, straight like that. So treat him the way you would me."

"That's law. If anyone has an issue with it, you come to me," her mom said. "Marvin, Taz, and Keasha, y'all come with me. Reggie, TK, and PJ you're welcome to anything in my house. Marcus, Kevin, Measha, Jeremy, and Jaleesa, y'all stay. Everyone else can leave and we'll bring you up to date tomorrow."

She led Taz and Kiki to a room made into an office. Taz now saw where Kiki got her commanding attitude from. He also saw where she got her shape.

There were only three chairs available, but before her dad could go get another seat, Kiki crawled in Taz's lap, making her mother grin.

"Are y'all sure y'all ain't girlfriend and boyfriend?" Her mother smiled.

"It's not like that," he said.

"Okay, listen, Keasha, I know you want some answers, so go ahead and ask away."

"How is Measha my twin? I don't remember her. And why did y'all leave me with that pedophile? Furthermore, I don't remember none of these dudes you call my brother - or you, for that matter," Kiki said, looking to her pops.

"Y'all were too young to remember me," he said, speaking for the first time. He had a heavy Atlanta twang. "I was around up until you were four, then I caught a drug charge and got twenty years."

"The reason you don't remember Measha is because we split y'all up when your father got locked up. All his so-called friends teamed up with his enemies and started killing any and everybody who stayed loyal. I kept you because you were the more sensitive of the two and you needed me. And right before I got locked up, I seen the wife of one of your father's main enemies that was trying to move into our territory and I cut her throat. It was really a war then. Then I caught the dude that set your father up and I killed him in the projects in front of everybody. They gave me seventeen years."

"Why do you keep calling your uncle a pedophile?" her dad asked.

Taz felt Kiki tense up in his lap and he started rubbing her back, trying to ease her nerves.

"He molested me. He used to make me jack him off. When Aunt Jackie died, he started touching me. I was only ten years old. The only thing he didn't do was put his dick in me, so why you think?" Kiki snapped.

"He dead now, so it don't even matter," Taz spoke up.

"And how come y'all never came looking for me?" Kiki asked.

"Baby, we have! Ever since we've been home, we've been trying to find you. Nobody knew anything. Ever since your uncle got killed, you've been off the map. After that day, nobody had heard from or seen you," her mom said. Then she turned her head to the side and squinted her eyes. "Did you do it?"

"No, he did. He had come to rob him and caught him making me jack his dick. I've been with him ever since."

"So what do you do for a living?" her dad asked

"Rob."

"Well, you don't have to do that anymore. We run Atlanta legally and illegally. We have quite a few businesses and we supply eighty percent of the drugs that come into the city. But I want you in the office with me," her mother told her. "I run an investigation firm and I have a spot for you. After you learn the ropes, you can pull in as much as seven figures a year."

"I'm not the office type, and besides, I never said I was moving down here," she explained.

"Well, you are" Mrs. Kiana informed her.

"Ha, ha, ha. How about not," Kiki responded.

Mother and daughter had a stare-off. This was going to be interesting, Taz thought.

"Keasha, you might not want to play with me," she warned. "I see you can handle a pistol and all, but where do you think you got that fire in your blood from? Me! Anything you've done or thought about doing, I've done! I've tortured and killed niggas! I see the worst of the worst! I'm the real Cookie from *Empire*. I run this shit! I built this shit from the ground up, I'm built like that, so try me."

"Consider it done." Kiki stood up and walked out.

"Oh, I'm about to show this heifer." Her mama stood up.

Taz and her dad just looked at each other. They both knew it was about to get ugly for somebody.

Nicholas Lock

Chapter 23

"So what, you think you grown?" Kiki's mom asked, walking behind her.

"Y'all ready?" Kiki asked Reggie, PJ, and TK, ignoring her question.

They had all gotten comfortable in the kitchen. PJ and TK were drinking beers while Reggie was eating a bowl of cereal.

"Did you hear me?" Her mom grabbed her shoulder and Kiki shrugged her off.

"Don't touch me!" She turned to face her mom.

She slapped Kiki across the face. Before Taz could get to her, Kiki fired on her mama. Taz had seen that same punch knock plenty of broads out, but her mother ate it and rushed her. She hit Kiki with a swift two-piece, then Taz grabbed Kiki.

"Hell no, let me go!" she screamed as everybody came to the kitchen to see what the commotion was about.

"Nah, shorty, that's your mom."

"Fuck that! She ain't raise me! She left me to fend for myself!"

"You better watch your mouth," Measha said.

"You can get it too, bitch!" Kiki got louder and Taz knew she was almost to the point of no return. He had to get her out of there.

"Taz, let her go, we about to settle this. I'm going to give her what you never did: a good ass whooping."

"We about to go," Taz said.

As much as Taz wanted to, he couldn't. He didn't think it was possible, but if she did happen to get off on Kiki, he didn't know how he would handle it. Mom or not, he didn't play the radio when it came to Kiki. Her father got him to change his mind.

"Let them get it out their system. It's the only way they're going to have an understanding. Two real alphas can't be around each other. Somebody has to submit. Let them have it out," he spoke some wisdom.

Taz looked in Kiki's eyes and saw that fire. He shook his head and put her down. As soon as her feet touched the floor, she shot after her mom. Mrs. Kiana waited until she got close, then side stepped and punched Kiki, in the jaw sending her to the floor. Reggie's, TK's, and PJ's jaw dropped. Bitches didn't do Kiki like that. Niggas didn't even do her like that.

She got up, looked at Taz, and rushed her again. Kiki was expecting the sidestep again, but instead, Mrs. Kiana met her head on. They got to fighting like Ali and Frasier, but Taz could tell Kiki was outmatched. Her mother was no joke! She swooped and scooped Kiki off her feet and got on top of her. She got two hits in and then Taz stepped in. He wasn't about to let Kiki get pounded. He grabbed her mama and pulled her off Kiki and Reggie grabbed Kiki.

"Reggie, if you don't let me go!"

He looked to Taz, knowing she would buck on him too.

Taz passed her mom off to her husband and grabbed Kiki. She knew no matter what, Taz didn't care about her trying to buck.

"You better get off me," Mrs. Kiana said icily and her husband immediately let her go.

Taz wasn't letting Kiki go until she calmed down. He wasn't her daddy and he wasn't bowing down. It was clear to see that her mother wore the pants in their relationship. Taz didn't mind if his woman wanted to rule with him, but rule by his side, not in front of him.

"That's dead! It's over," Taz told Mrs. Kiana as she walked toward him and Kiki.

She stopped and looked at him with a glare that he

matched. She wasn't going to cow him. He was the definition of the alpha male. His whole vibe said it. It was what a lot of women said attracted them to him. Everybody wasn't a boss, but he was, and she needed to know that. She smirked and walked out of the room.

"Let's go," he said.

As they were leaving, they had to pass Kiki's twin. She made the mistake of smacking her teeth as Kiki walked by and Kiki slapped her so hard she fell to one knee. Kiki bent down beside her and whispered, "I'm nothing like these hoes you been dealing with. I'm the last of a dying breed."

As they left, Taz saw her mom at the top of the stairs, smiling.

The next morning Taz and Kiki went to the Waffle House to have breakfast. Reggie, TK, and PJ stayed in bed because after they left Kiki's people's house, they went back to Magic City and Taz and Kiki went to the room.

"I guess the lick over now, huh?" Taz asked, sitting down at the table.

"I honestly don't know. My feelings are all over the place. A part of me is happy that I finally got some closure. Another part is like fuck them. Then that woman that calls herself my mother got me all the way fucked up! Something funny?" she asked, seeing Taz grinning.

"She busted your ass." He laughed "But that's not what's funny. What's funny is that you don't see that y'all are the exact same person. I see where you get it from now." He took a bite out of his biscuit.

"Whatever. And I see the way you was looking at her and that bitch Measha. I know you and you better not," she warned.

"Not what?"

Keasha didn't answer. She just raised her brow.

"Well, well, well. Speak of the devil." Taz looked out into the parking lot as Mrs. Kiana and Measha got out of a red Porsche.

"You ready?" Kiki asked, having not taken one bite of her All-Star meal.

"Hell no! I'm finishing this and that." He used his fork to point at his and her plate.

Kiki sat back, but huffed and crossed her arms across her chest.

All eyes were on Mrs. Kiana and Measha as they made their way straight to where they were sitting. They were dressed to the nines. Mrs. Kiana wore a white Vera Wang wool top and trousers and white Isabel Mormont leather boats. Measha was just as fly in a burgundy Gucci Pal Valeri turtleneck, tan self-portrait pants, and burgundy Gucci flats.

"Taz, Keasha." Mrs. Kiana approached "Can we sit down?"

Taz stood up and let her mother slide in beside him.

"Sucker," Kiki mumbled under her breath as she let Measha in.

True to form, Kiki's mother took control. "I thought about last night and I handled it the wrong way. I should've given you a choice. I just want you with me. I want to be able to catch up on all the things we missed. Am I wrong?"

Kiki shrugged her shoulders.

"Look, Keasha, you and your nonchalant attitude, you can miss me with that. It's taking a lot for me to even do this shit like this, but keep it up and we gon' have an issue, believe that," Mrs. Kiana warned.

Taz could feel the heat coming off her.

"You know Kiki not gon' leave her baby." Taz tried to lighten the mood.

"Who her baby?" her mom asked.

"Me."

"Nigga, you stupid." Kiki laughed and threw her napkin at him.

"For real though, I been thinking about moving and I ain't decided on whether it's going to be here or Miami. And it's a good chance wherever I go, Kiki going too."

"You have a real hold on my daughter. I don't know what you did to my baby, but it's obvious you have her loyalty," her mother stated.

"Tongue and hard dick," Measha misspoke.

"That's the difference between a bitch like me and a bitch like you. A nigga can get your loyalty for some lies and some good sex, while niggas can only get mine through blood, sweat, and tears. You get wet while laying on your back, but I get wet from putting niggas on they back. Just so you know, TWIN," she put emphasis on the word, "my cherry ain't been popped." She got up and walked out, leaving Taz with her mom and him, wondering why she had lied to him.

***

"So what's the plan?" Reggie asked, looking over at Taz. "Are we going to set up shop down here or what?" They were on the phone, going back to Fayetteville.

"You got to ask Kiki," he said.

After Kiki walked out of the Waffle House and cooled off, she came back in and she and her mother hashed things out. Not so much so with her and Measha. They came to an understanding. Kiki was going to start coming to Atlanta more often and vice versa so they could catch up. Taz was going to say something to Kiki about her being a virgin, but he thought better of it.

"So what it's going to be, Keasha?" PJ asked.

She looked at him and said, "I been giving this shit a lot of thought. So I got a question for y'all before I answer. What if we come together and got money together? Before y'all argue, just listen to my logic. They have the whole city locked up. Yeah, there may be some who aren't all the way content with OTF, but for the most part, everyone is. We don't have the manpower or the money to go to war with them. Maybe in our city we do, but definitely not on their home turf.

"But we can get a lot of their people to switch sides, especially with the quality of our work and prices," TK commented.

"I don't doubt it. But do you really want them kind of people on your team? Because obviously their loyalty can be bought. So what happens when someone comes along with better work and prices? Furthermore, I've never seen a war that didn't result in casualties. I don't know about y'all, but I'm not trying to lose anybody. So I say we team up and run it up without the risk of lives, plus we can let them do most of the work and reap the fruits of their labor. And keep in mind they're blood too."

Taz smiled. Kiki was on her shit. They didn't have to ask his opinion. They already knew he was going to let Kiki have her way. He looked at PJ, Reggie, and TK, and they were all nodding their head in agreement. This was perfect, because once they set this move up, he was going to go ahead and start falling back from the game and move into his business ventures.

Chapter 24

"Baby, I need to talk to you," Isabella said, lying on Taz's stomach.

They had just got done with an intense fuck session and Taz was trying to go to sleep. He really wasn't trying to talk.

"What's up?" His eyes remaining closed.

"You're going to have to kill Pablo."

"Why you say that?" he asked, even though he'd already had it in his mind to do just that.

"Because if you don't, he's going to kill you," she said matter-of-factly. "I know him, and he's not going to let that shit die. My brother knows it too. That's why he sent him back to Mexico. But he's going to come back, and when he does, it's going to be an issue. So I need you to do what needs to be done because if you don't, I will. Plus I refuse to be a single mother."

Hearing this, Taz's eyes popped open. He looked at Isabella and she was smiling. She crawled up his body until they were face to face.

"Yeah, you're going to be a daddy a third time."

"When did you find out?" He sat up.

"Yesterday. I took a pregnancy test and it was positive. I think I'm about five weeks," she confessed.

"You told your dad yet?"

"No, but I will today." She was beaming. "He's been wanting grandkids."

"It's about time I got me a boy."

"A boy? No, boo, it's going to be a girl."

Taz shook his head at her comment. His mind started going into overdrive. He had to do something about the Pablo situation. Then he had to tie up the loose ends as far as his exit from the game. That would free him up to expand his legal

173

workings and decide where he was going to raise his family. Atlanta was a major possibility, but the prospect of yearlong summers was getting too appealing to turn down.

"How you feel about moving, Bella?" he asked, pulling her onto his lap.

"I don't care. Wherever you go, I'm going." She put her head on his chest.

"I been thinking about Atlanta or Miami."

"I like Miami, and Atlanta is the one place I'm not moving to."

"Why not, bae?" He rubbed on her butt.

"I just don't like it.

"Miami it is then. You need to go ahead and start getting your affairs together for this move then. And tell your dad I need to holler at him about something too."

"Okey, baby."

"Now can I get some sleep now?"

She nodded her head and got comfortable as they went to sleep in each other's arms.

***

"What's happening, Allison?" Taz asked, walking into her office.

"Nothing." She smiled.

Taz was at the bank getting another loan for two foreclosed houses that had caught his eye. With a little minor repair and cosmetic work, Taz estimated he was going to make a quarter million dollars profit. The two houses he was acquiring were worth at least two hundred thousand a piece, but he was buying them both for two hundred thousand total. He had already set up appointments to get the kitchen and bathrooms remodeled in one and the other one he was getting a new roof put on and new windows installed, which would increase the value in both.

"Oh, if you would just sign these papers, you'll be all set to go," Allison told Taz, pushing the papers towards him.

"What exactly does this mean?"

Allison came from around the desk to see what Taz was pointing at. She leaned over, giving Taz a clear view of her D-cups. As she explained, Taz only half listened as her breasts had his undivided attention.

"You have some pretty fucking titties," he blurted out.

"Excuse me?"

"Let me see your titties." He threw caution to the wind.

She just stared at him with her mouth hanging open and her eyes wide open in disbelief.

"You better close your mouth before I put something in it."

Allison closed her mouth so fast her teeth clicked. Seeing she hadn't kicked him out yet, he was going to see how far she was going to let him go.

"You see what you're doing to me?" Taz took ahold of her hand and put it in his lap on top of his rapidly hardening dick. When she squeezed, he knew she was too far gone. He stood up, closed the blinds to her office, and locked the door.

"What are you doing?" she asked as if coming to her senses.

Instead of saying anything, Taz started unbuckling his slacks, causing her eyes to get big again.

"What are you doing?" she repeated.

Taz dropped his pants, pulled his dick out, and walked towards where she was standing. The more Taz walked her way, the more she backed up until she was against her desk. Her eyes were locked onto his dick as he approached her. He ripped her blouse open, sending buttons flying everywhere. Taz looked down at her breasts and her nipples were at full attention. He leaned down and sucked one into his mouth, causing her to cry out. He lifted her up and sat her on the edge of the desk. Reaching under her skirt, Taz ripped her thong off and put it in his pocket. He looked Allison in the face as he rubbed his dick up and down her dripping wet pussy.

"Put it in," Taz said, letting go.

Allison wrapped her legs around his waist and guided him inside her sugar walls.

"Ssss," she moaned as he slid inside her.

Taz pushed her back so that she was on her back, then placed her legs on his shoulders and went to work.

"Oh shit!" Allison said when he pushed all the way in.

"You better hush before somebody comes to the door." Taz continued to dig deep.

If Taz would've known snow bunnies were giving it up like this, he would've been taking them down. He reached down and started playing with Allison's clit and she lost it.

"Yes! Yes!" she screamed, making Taz stop. He reached in his shirt pocket, pulled her thong out, and stuffed it in her mouth, then went back to stuffing her. He watched as her love juices coated his dick. He was loving not only the noises her pussy was making, but the contrast of her pale skin against his dark skin.

"Mmm!" she moaned through the thong as she started to cum all over his dick.

When she calmed down, Taz pulled her to her feet and pushed her down on her knees. She didn't need coaxing. She went to work on his dick like her life depended on it. She was giving Taz that porno head. She was rubbing his dick all over her face, slapping it on her tongue, the whole nine.

"I'm about to bust," he told her and she pulled him to the

back of her throat and swallowed all his kids.

Taz fixed his clothes and just stared at her as she tried to fix herself up, but there was no fixing her blouse, so she put her jacket on.

"We most definitely going to do this in the near future," Taz said, making her blush and nod her head.

He signed the papers and walked out of her office, only to see Tyshae standing in the doorway of her office with her arms crossed and a scowl on her face.

Not wanting to hear her mouth, he just kept walking out of the bank. He'd call her later.

Nicholas Lock

Chapter 25

"Baby, my daddy is going to be in town today," Isabella informed Taz.

They had just left the doctor's office and he confirmed that Isabella was seven weeks pregnant. While she was all giddy and excited, Taz was mellower. He'd been through all that the first two times when he had his daughters. Isabella turned a forty-five minute visit into an hour and a half with all the questions she asked. Taz wasn't tripping. He let her enjoy herself, since it was her first child.

"Tell him I want to meet him at the same time that I meet with your brother to get this work."

"I'm coming too."

"No, you're not. You're going to stay at home with my daughters and take care of my baby." He put his hand on her stomach. "What your dad say about you being pregnant?"

She put her hand on top of his. "He's happy. He said now I'll have to sit down somewhere, but he's mistaken."

"Oh, you most definitely going to be sitting your ass down. Just as soon as we get everything took care of, we going to Miami to look for houses."

"If that's what you think…"

Taz looked over at her. He knew it was going to be hell getting her stubborn ass to sit down, but once he got her to Miami, she wouldn't have too much of a choice. In the meantime, he had to make sure this meeting went according to plan. He called Kiki.

"Yo, I want you and TK to come with me when I meet the plug. I'm about to try to put TK in the driver's seat," Taz told Kiki when she answered the phone.

"I'll be there. Just tell me when and where. We also need to hit ATL so we can see where we going to set up shop at. I talked to my mom and she's with us expanding down there as long as it keeps me close by."

"We? No, y'all. That's why I'm putting TK in the driver's seat, I'm done with that side. Don't get me wrong though, I'll be around to give my advice on certain situations, but as for being involved in the day to day side of things, nah, that's dead. You need to be doing the same thing.

"Yeah, yeah, yeah," she said sarcastically.

"A'ight, whatever. Four-thirty, Micasita's. Bye." He hung up.

"Bae, you cooking tonight?" he asked, but didn't get an answer. When he looked over at her she had her arms crossed, eyes squinted and lips poked out. He cracked up laughing.

"What's wrong, Bella?" He already knew.

"Why you need her to go and not me?"

"Is somebody jealous?" he teased.

"Don't play yourself, boo boo. I got you. You sleep beside me every night, you eat this pussy whenever I say, and I'm about to have your baby. Jealous? Never."

"You need to step your shit. That's my sister, girl, of course you ain't got no reason to be jealous or threatened." He tried to kiss her on the cheek and she moved her face.

"But she's not your blood sister. Tyshae is."

"That blood shit is overrated."

"Blood is thicker than water," she said.

"But loyalty is thicker than blood," he shot right back, shutting her up for good.

***

"Okay, this is how it's going down. Kiki, your ass don't need to say nothing. Just watch my back. And TK, you gon' have to be on your shit because he might grill you. I'm going to put a good word in, but I don't have the final say. If all else fails, I'll get Isabella to throw her weight around. Speaking of Isabella, me, you, and her are going out to eat. Kiki and y'all are going to settle these issues. I can't have y'all beefing."

"I'm not thinking about your bitch! As long as she plays her position, I won't have to rearrange her dental plan."

"Don't play with me, Keasha, she carrying my baby, so you can nix the idea of putting your hands on her," he warned and she rolled her eyes.

They pulled into Micasita's, preventing Kiki from making an off the wall comment. As soon as they stepped out of Taz's CT6, he saw Pablo shooting daggers in his direction. Taz matched Pablo's stare.

"Something on your mind?" Pablo stated when Taz walked up, causing Kiki and TK to grip.

Taz shook his head to calm them and then told Pablo, "I'm just thinking about how your brains are going to look decorating the wall."

Taz walked past him into the restaurant with Kiki and TK on his heels. Juan greeted him with a handshake and led him to the back where his father was. Taz's temperature shot through the roof when he walked into the office and saw Isabella sitting against the wall.

"I thought I told you to stay your ass at home," he said.

"And I didn't want to." She folded her arms, making it worse.

"We see who wears the pants in the house," Pablo joked, making Taz even madder.

"One word! Just one more fucking word! And I'm going to put a hole so big in you Jesus is not going to be able to save you!" Taz warned through gritted teeth.

Pablo was about to open his mouth, but Hector put his hand up, stopping him.

"Isabella, go home, I'm so serious."

"No," she whined, poking her lips out.

"I got a trick for your ass," Taz said, then turned to her dad, who was looking back and forth from Taz to Isabella with a grin on his face.

"She's her mother's daughter. I used to have the same issues with her mother. You have to put some of the blame on me, Taz. Her whole life all she's ever heard was yes. No one has ever really told her what to do," informed Hector.

"Let's get to why we're here," Taz said, not in the mood for small talk. "Listen, you took a chance on me and I didn't disappoint. Like you, I've moved into the legal side of business, and it's becoming quite lucrative. I say all that to say this: I'm about to fall back from the drug game, but my man right here is who I want to take my place."

"Okay," he said, taking Taz by surprise at how easy it was. "But remember this: you're responsible for the actions of whoever you vouch for. Now that that's out of the way, I thank you for making me a grandfather. I've been telling them for years I want to have some grandkids to spoil. This makes you family," Hector said.

Taz started thinking over Hector's last statement, wondering how far being family was going to allow him to push the boundaries. Because what he had in mind was going to test that theory to the fullest extent. "And who is this pretty lady? For some reason, she looks very familiar, I just can't say from where," Hector stated.

"Dad, I was thinking the same thing," Juan said.

"This is my sister Kiki. Kiki, this is Hector and his son Juan. You already know Isabella."

Isabella snarled, causing her dad to look her way.

"I have a question for you. I've been thinking about it for the last few minutes," Taz said.

"What?" asked Hector.

"Family is precious, correct? And you side with family whether they're right or wrong, right?"

"Yes, of course," Hector said, not understanding where Taz was going with his line of questioning.

Hearing his answer, Taz pulled his gun, turned to Pablo, and put two hollow points in his head, sending blood and brain matter all over the wall. While everyone else flinched, Kiki and Hector didn't bat an eye. Hector just raised a brow and shrugged. Taz looked at Juan to see his reaction and he was staring at his childhood friend's body, which gave Taz some concern.

"He was becoming a loose end. We were going to have to handle him sooner or later," Hector said more to his son than to anybody else.

With that, Taz walked out, but not before giving Isabella a look that said she was in for it.

Nicholas Lock

Chapter 26

"You just don't listen! I told you not to mess with my homegirl, but you did it anyway Mr. I-don't-do-snow-bunnies," Tyshae blanked.

"I ain't come over here to hear all that, Shae. That woman grown, and you not going to have to worry about it too much longer because I'm about to move to Miami," he informed her.

"And when exactly where you planning on telling me?"

"I just did, Shae. But the question is, are you coming or not?"

"To Miami?"

"Nah, Africa. Yeah, Miami."

"I'd have to put in a transfer, get some movers, and find a place to stay."

"You making a big deal of nothing. We can take care of all that easily. Just think of all the money we going to make off foreclosed homes and businesses down there." He tried influencing her decision.

"When are you going?"

"As soon as I wrap up all my business, which'll probably be in the next week or so. There's no rush though. Whenever you get your stuff in order, I'll be waiting."

"I'll be ready in about a month."

"Well, I'm going to holler at you later. I got some shit to handle," Taz said, giving Tyshae a hug and leaving.

When he got in his car, he called Keishana.

"Hey, boo!" she answered.

"You at home?"

"Yeah, why?" asked Keishana

"I'm about to come through." He hung up.

Taz was tying up all his loose ends before he left for Miami. He had already picked the house without Isabella's help. He hadn't talked to her since she pulled that stunt at Micasita's. She had been blowing his phone up, but he was ignoring her. Taz was really starting to second guess fucking with her. He was a firm believer in the man being the head of the household, but she was acting like she was the head. Taz had no problem with his woman calling shots, but when he said something, he expected his lady to follow his lead. He wasn't planning on speaking to her until he came back from his trip to Atlanta. By then, he hoped she had her act together. If not, she was going to find herself in Fayetteville while he was in Miami.

"Damn!" Taz said when he saw Mary's car in Keishana's driveway. He had forgotten to get at her when he got back.

Before Taz could knock, Keishana answered the door, looking good as ever.

"What's up, boy?" She gave him a hug.

"You." He cuffed her ass. Taz walked into the living room and sat down beside Mary and she scooted to the other side.

"Bitch, stop fronting!" Keishana told Mary.

Taz grabbed Mary and pulled her onto his lap.

"Let me go, Taz."

"You mad at me? My bad, girl, I really been busy as hell, but you got my word that before I move, I'm going to give you a whole day."

"Move where?" asked Mary

"Miami."

"Oh shit! Speaking of Miami, that nigga Zion been blowing my phone up. I been ignoring that shit though. I'm about to get my number changed," Keishana told Taz.

He had really forgotten about the nigga, to be truthful, but since he was moving to Miami, he might have to go ahead and take care of the nigga and his son, especially considering what happened the last time he was there.

"This him right here," Keishana said, looking at her phone.

"Give me the phone," Taz said. "Hello."

"Bitch, mi gon' - who dis?" Zion asked.

"Well, well, well, somebody sounds upset," Taz teased.

"Taz? Ya bombaclot!"

"Why all the name calling? If anybody should be calling names it should be me, since Gutta is still breathing."

"Ya sent dat dirty bitch to mi? And she gave mi and mi son HIV," Zion said more to himself than to Taz.

"Y'all should've held up your end of the bargain and this wouldn't have happened, but…"

"It's okay, fuck boi! Laugh now, but cry lata," Zion said and then he hung up, leaving Taz with a little hint of worry since he knew Zion wasn't to be taken lightly.

"Why you can't chill with me today?" asked Mary, turning to face him. "Oh, what, your girl got you on lock?"

"You going to get some time with daddy. You ain't got to be jealous," Taz said while dialing Kiki's number.

"I want to watch," Keishana said.

"What you want, nigga?" Kiki answered.

"We need some plans on taking care of Zion and Gutta yesterday."

"Say no more. Now bye, I'm busy." She hung up.

"When you moving?" asked Mary.

"If everything goes according to plan, in the next few weeks."

"I got to start packing then," Keishana said.

"I already knew you was going to want to come with me," he laughed. "I think I'll be able to find a job for you because I'm thinking about starting my own real estate business, and don't nothing make niggas spend money like a fat ass and pretty face."

"What about me?" Mary pouted.

"Are you going to behave? Because my bitch ain't going for no dumb shit."

"I got you, nigga."

"A'ight, we going to see, but the minute you get on that other shit, it's over," he told her. "Now show your girl how you be riding this dick."

Taz fucked Mary right there on the couch with Keishana watching and playing with her pussy.

***

"I'm glad y'all could meet with me on such short notice," Taz told Olivia and Victoria.

They were at the office, which was unusually quiet for a Monday afternoon. His original plan was to let them know he was relocating to Miami, but then a thought occurred to him - one that would prove lucrative.

"I called this meeting to let y'all know that I'm about to move to Miami, but in the process of trying to figure out how I was going to work this out, an idea popped in my head. How do y'all feel about expanding and opening a store in Miami?"

"We were just discussing the benefits of opening a new store. But who would run it?" Olivia asked.

"One of you would need to come down to get it up and running, but after that, I could handle the day to day operations."

"What you think, Vicky?" Olivia wanted her sister's opinion.

"I'm all for it, but which one of us is going to go down there to get things up and running?"

"I wouldn't mind going to Miami and getting a tan," Olivia said.

"Who do you think should go, D'angelo?" Victoria asked him with a raised brow.

Taz took the diplomatic approach and said, "I'll let y'all decide that amongst yourselves, being that you guys know who's better qualified."

Victoria and Olivia looked at each other and Taz stood up to leave.

"There's no rush. You still have a few weeks to decide and I still have to get a few more affairs in order before I go anyhow."

"D'angelo, can I have a word with you before you leave?" Victoria asked as Olivia walked out.

"What's up, Vicky?" He sat on the edge of the conference table.

"We aren't going to have any issues between us, are we?"

"That's what you wanted to talk to me about? I thought you had a real problem," he said, standing up. "No, we not going to have no issues. The only issue we going to have is if you don't bring this pussy to Miami." He slapped her on the ass and walked out, leaving her bright red.

Taz's next step was Primo's Pizza. Taz approached Mr. Tessatore with the same proposition he came to Victoria and Olivia with. He agreed before Taz could get the words out of his mouth. He was going to send his son to run the business. That way, Taz wouldn't be stretching himself too thin.

The only thing left to do was deal with the Zoe Pound Mafia once and for all, then his work would be complete.

And Taz thought he had just the plan to take care of Zion and Gutta.

Nicholas Lock

Chapter 27

Taz had just dropped his daughters off at Tyshae's house when Isabella's cherry-red Mercedes cut him off. She stuck her head out the window and yelled "Pull the fuck over!"

He thought about ignoring her, but he didn't know what lengths she was going to go to in order to get his attention. Taz still hadn't talked to her since the meeting with her father. He pulled over at a Kangaroo gas station and got out as Isabella swerved in behind him. The car had barely come to a stop and she was already out of the car and charging in his direction. She wasted no time. When she got in reach, she started raining down blows on him.

"Why the fuck you ain't been home? Why you didn't answer your phone?" She continued to punch on him.

"Stop fucking hitting me!" Taz yelled, grabbing her arms. "You ain't got the right to question me! You don't fucking listen. I told your ass to stay the hell home and what did you do?" He shook her.

"Take your hands off her," some white dude said.

"Mind your fucking business!" Taz said.

Before Taz could react, the man hit him in the side of the head, causing him to let Isabella go and stumble against his car.

"He told you to mind your business, so that's what the hell you need to do." Isabella thrust her ever-present .380 in his face.

He threw his hands up and backed away "You got it, Miss."

"Put that gun up, Bella," Taz told her as the dude got in his car and sped away.

"I should shoot you," she admitted, tucking her gun away.

"Now take your ass home, Bella."

"Not unless you bring your ass with me."

"That's the shit I be talking about right there! You don't listen to shit I say! And you wonder why I ain't been home?" Taz blanked, rubbing his hand down his face.

"You know what? Fuck you!" She stormed off towards her car.

As Taz turned to get in his car, she called his name. He started not to turn around, but something in her voice caught his attention. His face fell when he turned around. There stood Gutta and four other dread heads, and Gutta had a gun pointed at Isabella's head. Taz knew he didn't have a shot in hell of reaching her before Gutta did.

"Zion said laugh now, cry lata, and it's lata." Gutta shot Isabella in the face.

"Nooo!" Taz yelled.

He started letting off, hitting one dude in the chest, but their barrage of bullets sent him ducking behind his car. He peeked around the car as Gutta was getting in a black SUV. Taz immediately went to check on Isabella. There was blood all over her head, but she was still breathing.

"Just hold on, baby."

Taz scooped her up and carried her to his car. He swerved out of the gas station, rushing her to the hospital. On the way, he called Kiki and told her to meet him at the hospital, then he made a call he dreaded. He called Hector and told him Isabella had gotten shot and he was taking her to the hospital. After he told him which hospital, he hung up. He didn't let the car stop before he scooped Isabella up and carried her into the ER. He didn't have to say a word. When the nurses saw him carrying a bleeding Isabella, they took her from him and rushed her straight to the back. They refused to let Taz follow them, so he paced back and forth in the waiting room.

"What the fuck?" Kiki asked, coming into the waiting

room, seeing Taz covered in blood.

"Gutta shot Isabella in the head."

Kiki's eyes got big and she put her hand over her mouth in shock. Before Taz could begin to tell her what happened, Hector and all his bodyguards strolled into the waiting room.

"Where the fuck is my daughter?" he bassed.

"They took her in the back."

"Who shot her?" Hector asked borderline hysterical.

"I'm going to handle it," Taz told him.

"You better. If not, I'm going to handle you," he warned, walking off.

One of the nurses that had taken Isabella in the back came out and walked up to Taz. "Are you her family?"

"Yes, that's my child's mother."

"She's extremely lucky. The bullet only grazed her temple. There's no structural damage and the baby is fine. She's sedated right now, but you'll be able to see her when we get her settled in a room."

"Why was there so much blood?" Taz wanted to know.

"All head wounds bleed excessively," informed the nurse.

"What's going on?" Hector asked, walking back up.

Taz filled him in on what the nurse had told him and he could see Hector visibly relax. Since her injuries weren't life-threatening, Taz was able to breathe easier. After he told Hector the update, he went in the corner and got on the phone while Taz paced back and forth.

"Sit down, you driving me crazy," Kiki said.

He looked her way and kept pacing without saying a word.

"Mr. Walker, you can see her now." The nurse led them to Isabella's room.

Taz's breath got caught up in his chest at his first look at Isabella. She looked so fragile laying up in the bed with the IV in her hand. The side of her head where the bullet had grazed her had been shaved bald, but other than that, she looked okay. He walked up to the side of her bed and grabbed her hand.

"I got you, boo, just worry about getting better," he said as a tear fell from his eye.

Taz turned and walked out without even a glance in her dad's direction.

Kiki was standing outside the door. She hadn't come into the room. Taz looked at her and said "We about to make Miami real bloody."

Taz wasted no time. He and Kiki were on a flight out to Miami the very next day. They touched down that night and checked into the Hilton. There were two bags on the bed when they walked into the room. Taz opened them and whistled. Kiki's mom had come through. The bags were filled with guns. There was everything from HTK.45's to AR15's. There was even a Taser X26P, which was supposed to be one of the most powerful Taser's to date. They changed and headed out.

Gutta was known to frequent a Haitian Club in downtown Miami called Top Shoota's. Since they still hadn't figured out what his relationship was with Agent Evans, they couldn't afford any slip-ups. They weren't trying to have another Quadree incident. The club was their only real option. They wanted to catch him at his house, but he'd moved, so this was their only real chance at catching up to him without too much chaos.

"We going in or what?" Kiki asked.

Taz looked at her like she was crazy. "This is a Haitian club, so ask yourself, how many Zoe Pound niggas do you think are inside? I don't believe in committing suicide."

"So we just going to sit out here and wait?" Kiki was getting frustrated.

"Pretty much. When he comes out, we going to put these

hot balls in him and whatever dread head that gets in the way."

"Whatever you say," she huffed.

"Hello," Taz answered his phone.

"You going to love me, nigga," Tyshae said.

"I'm busy, Shae, let me hit you back," he said, about to hang up.

"You better not hang this fucking phone up!"

"What, Shae?"

"Like I said, you going to love me. I'm going to kill Gutta for you," she said excitedly.

"You about too late for that," Taz said, glancing at the club entrance.

"How you figure that when the nigga been rubbing on my ass all night," she said, catching Taz off guard.

"Where the hell you at?"

"I'm in the bathroom at this club in Miami and we about to go back to his house."

"No, Tyshae! I'm outside right now, so get the fuck out of there!"

"Just chill, bro, I got this," she said and hung up.

"Fuck!"

"What's up?" asked Kiki.

"Tyshae in there talking about how she's going to kill Gutta for me. We got to do something. Shae not built like that."

"Oh. My. God."

Before they could come up with a plan, Gutta and Tyshae came out of the club followed by ten dread heads.

"Fuck, Shae!" Taz pounded the steering wheel.

Taz could only watch as his sister got in a truck with Gutta and took off.

"Nah, fuck that!" Taz started following them, but a roadblock held them up just long enough that they lost them.

"She going to be good," Kiki said, seeing the worry on Taz's face.

Taz had no choice but to go back to the hotel and wait for Tyshae to call him. It didn't take long. Two hours later, her name came across his caller ID.

"Where you at?"

"Did ya tink mi fall fa da some ting again?" Gutta's voice came through, hitting Taz in the gut. "Da only difference was dis time mi an all mi boys took a turn, den mi kill da bitch! Ya want da bitch back, she at 113 Mercury Drive. Ya next, pussy boi!"

Taz took off out the door with Kiki on his heels. They got in the truck and Taz put the address in the GPS without a word. Sensing his mood, Kiki didn't say anything. They rode in silence. They pulled up to an abandoned house in little Haiti. Taz kicked the door in and ran in with his gun drawn, not caring if it was a trap or not.

Tyshae was in the back room naked, sprawled out on a dirty mattress. She was covered in blood. Taz knelt down beside her to check her pulse and she opened her eyes.

"I'm sorry," she whispered and then closed her eyes a final time.

"No, Shae!" Taz said, but she was gone. "Ahhh!" He broke down crying, rocking Tyshae in his arms.

Chapter 28

Taz was sending Tyshae away in style. He bought an all-white casket trimmed in gold. Her name was airbrushed all over the casket and her portrait was drawn on top. Kiki picked the outfit, and he had no complaints. Kiki had put Shae in a white Chanel blouse and white Chanel pants. She looked like the angel that she was. The turnout for her funeral wasn't what Taz expected.

The church was packed to capacity. Taz looked around and he was more than sure that half the people in attendance didn't even know Shae. He had half a mind to have most of them cut, but he didn't want to cause a scene. He looked around and locked eyes with Allison, and she mouthed the words "I'm sorry". Taz didn't doubt her sincerity, but he was tired of everyone offering their condolences. This wasn't how it was supposed to be. Zion was supposed to be getting the I'm sorry's, not Taz. This was new territory for him. He had never been on this side of the game. He caused funerals, not attended them! He was starting to think that maybe he'd bitten off more than he could chew. The Zoe Pound was turning into a formidable foe. As bad as Taz wanted to bow out, he wasn't going to be able to, especially now that they had killed his sister. The Zoe Pound was turning out to be ten times more lethal and ruthless than anybody he'd ever gone up against.

"You okay?" Isabella asked, rubbing his hand.

Taz nodded his head. Isabella was cleared to go home the next day since the bullet didn't penetrate. You'd have thought coming that close to death she'd be a little more subdued, but she was anything but. She was more unruly than ever. She had even started calling herself Teflon Bella. The upside of it, though, was she listened to him more, to a certain extent. The side of her head where the bullet grazed was shaved low, so she rocked it low on that side and long on the other. Taz liked it, but he'd be glad when it grew back. Since she had come home, her dad had assigned her a personal security detail until Taz handled the issue. Hector had offered to handle it, but like T.I. said, "my partners would've did the job for a flat fee, but seeing the nigga bleed the only thing that's going to relax me. I'm hands on, nigga, damn what you say." One thing Taz was sure of: he was going to have to handle the situation ASAP because there was no way he was moving his daughters to Miami with Zion and Gutta alive. Another plus that came out of the Isabella situation was hers and Kiki's relationship. They were being cordial. He just didn't know how long it was going to last.

As the pastor started his eulogy, Taz blocked him out and thought of all the good times he and Shae had growing up. He found himself smiling, thinking of the day Tyshae had blanked on him, saying he must've wanted her to be gay after he'd beaten another one of her boyfriends up.

Before Taz knew it, the eulogy was over and it was time to go to the burial site. He really wanted to skip this whole part. He was having a hard enough time keeping it together, but to see his baby sister get lowered into the ground might break the dam. Taz was supposed to be one of the pallbearers, but he let someone else take his place. The weather matched Taz's mood. It was a gloomy day with a slight drizzle.

"Daddy, we want to ride with you," his daughters said.

"Come on." He let them climb into the limo with him and Isabella.

Taz laid his head back and closed his eyes on the ride to the burial site. He still couldn't believe his sister was gone.

"Daddy, your hair looks better that his." D'Azia pointed out the window.

When Taz opened his eyes to see what his baby was

talking about, dread filled his insides. To the right of him was a truck full of Haitians. Then he turned to the left and saw the same thing. The tint prevented them from knowing that Taz was looking at them. Taz wondered what they were waiting on.

"Neveah, you and D'Azia get on the floor right now!" Taz said as he called Kiki in the truck behind them.

"What's up?" Isabella asked, alarmed, and he pointed to the two trucks on either side of them.

"You see these two trucks riding beside us?" Taz asked Kiki. "Well, they're full of Haitians. I need y'all to get them the fuck away from me and my daughters yesterday!"

"Say no more."

As soon as they hung up, he could see the dudes in the truck to the left getting ready to raise their guns, but Kiki and them beat them to the punch.

TAT! TAT! TAT! TAT! TAT! TAT!

Reggie leaned out the window with the AR15 and Kiki was leaning out the other one, shooting the MAC90. Seeing the situation unfold, Isabella's security detail joined in and eliminated any notion of doing harm to Taz or his family. They only accomplished messing up Tyshae's funeral. They left two bullet-riddled trucks behind as Bella and his daughters huddled under him. As Taz looked at the fear etched on his babies' faces, he made his mind up to take care of Zion and Gutta no matter the cost.

***

The past week and a half, Taz had been all out of whack. But in the process, he'd been trying to catch a break. He needed a way to deal with Zion and Gutta. He was going to just go for what he knew. When he saw either one, he was going to let the clip go. He didn't care where they were, be it in public or church! The rules of engagement were that there were no rules.

Taz was on his way to drop his daughters off at their mother's house when a car pulled up alongside him and started blowing the horn. He saw it was the chick he met at the club. She was telling him to pull over.

"What's up?" Taz asked when he pulled over.

"So you just forgot all about me, huh?" Nesha asked, getting out of her car, making Taz wonder how he'd forgotten.

She had on some white leggings that looked like she was born in them and a red sweater complimented her red dreads.

"Honestly, I've had so much going on I ain't had no time for self."

"I see. Your hair all fuzzy and shit. And I'm sorry about your sister," she offered her condolences.

"How you know about that?"

"Come on, Taz, everybody knows who you is, plus I been keeping tabs on you."

"You know, they got a charge for that. It's called stalking." He smiled.

"Boy, bye!" Nesha laughed. "So when we going to chill?"

"Give me a couple of days and I got you. What's your name again?"

She took Taz's phone and called hers. "That way if you don't call me, I'm going to call you."

"Bet." Taz watched her walk back to her car, ass moving everywhere but straight. He was definitely calling her when he got back.

"I'm going to tell Ms. Bella," Neveah said from the backseat.

"Go ahead and tell, but if you do, I'm sending you back to stay at your mama's and I'm not getting you nothing for your birthday," he said, causing her to sit back in her seat and D'Azia to laugh at her. Taz dropped his daughters off just as his phone rang.

"Hello."

"You won't believe who I'm looking at right now," Candace said.

"I don't get no 'hey Taz' or nothing?"

"Gutta is at the Jamaican spot on Murchison." She ignored his comment.

"Stop playing with me." Taz's adrenaline started pumping.

"Swear to God!"

Taz hung up and busted a U-turn, going back towards Murchison Road. If Candace was bullshitting, he was going to fuck her up. There was no way Gutta was in Fayetteville and just out in the open. Taz wasn't going to believe it until he saw it. He was glad he wasn't in the Ferrari, or he wouldn't have been able to get close.

As Taz approached the Jamaican restaurant, shots started ringing out.

BOOM! BOOM! BOOM! KAH! KAH! KAH! KAH!

Taz ducked down, thinking someone was shooting at him. But when he looked towards the restaurant, he saw Kiki and Isabella running and hopping in a black Camaro and speeding off.

"Fuck you got going on? And why the fuck you got Bella with you?" Taz yelled into the phone.

"First of all, quit yelling at me, and second of all, I'm with her. She came and got me when she saw Gutta and his goons," Kiki defended herself.

"Put her on the phone!"

"Yes, papi."

"Go home! Now!" Taz yelled, hanging up

Taz waited a little while and drove back by the restaurant

201

and saw the coroner loading up black body bags. Bella and Kiki had done what he couldn't do. But now he was about to show Zion how you really fucked a funeral up.

Chapter 29

Unlike the day of Tyshae's funeral, which was drizzling and gloomy, Gutta's was bright and sunny. But Taz had plans on changing the forecast.

Taz and Kiki had been in Miami for the last few days, trying to come up with a plan for taking Zion out of the game. The best option was the funeral, which was why they got to the funeral home when it first opened and tied the owner up. All they had to do now was wait for Zion and his entourage to show up. While they waited, an idea came to Taz. He went to the room in the back where they did cremations.

"Kiki, come here!" Taz yelled.

"Why the hell you hollering? You going to wake up the dead."

"I'd love for Gutta to get up. He'd just die a second time. But check this out." He pointed to the incinerator.

"Ain't that where they burn the bodies?" she asked, but then she knew exactly what Taz was thinking.

"Can you think of a more deserving death for Zion? To be burned alive."

"I need you to explain to me just how you plan on getting him inside without too much commotion," Kiki inquired.

"You think I give a damn about making some noise? This nigga the reason my baby sister is dead! When he steps foot inside this funeral home, it's instant action! I'll die before I let this pussy get away!" Taz didn't give Kiki a chance to respond. He went over to the incinerator and turned it all the way up.

"You know this nigga turned my whole life upside down!" Taz continued to rant. "My shit ain't been right since Quadree's bitch ass, then I had to put all my shit on hold because I refused to take my babies to Miami with these niggas alive. Then Tyshae went and got herself killed," Taz vented as tears started falling down his face.

"Hello!" They heard Zion's voice and they both froze. "Where da hell is dis guy at?" Zion asked, looking for the funeral director.

Taz and Kiki had to make a move before he stumbled across the director and raised the alarm.

"Fucking bombaclot!" They heard him say as they moved into the hallway.

Taz and Kiki rounded the corner just as Zion was rounding the corner and he and Taz crashed into each other, causing Taz's pistol to fly across the hall. Zion immediately went for the gun and Taz jumped on his back just as Zion grabbed hold of the pistol. Taz grabbed Zion's head and slammed it into the ground with all his might, knocking him out cold. Taz got the gun and stood up, expecting a shootout but all was quiet. When he looked at Kiki, she had a smirk on her face.

"Something funny?" Taz asked, looking towards the front of the funeral home.

"You falling off."

"All the more reason for me to leave this to the young boys. Where his people?"

"They all waiting outside. This ain't where the funeral was going to be, so he was probably just coming to check on things, expecting to be in and out. So he probably told them he was going to be right back," Kiki said.

"Good. That means we don't have much time. Grab his feet."

They carried Zion into the room where the incinerator was and as soon as they were loading him onto the pull-out rock, he came to. But by then it was too late. Taz pushed the rack in before Zion knew what was going on. The minute he was in, Taz closed the opening, but they could still hear his screams. Wasting no time, they slipped out the back and drove off, leaving Taz's problems behind him forever.

Four months later...

Since Gutta's and Zion's deaths, everything was smooth sailing. Taz had completed his move to Miami. The businesses were up and running and already turning over profits, TK's transition of taking over for Taz was a success, and Kiki was living right next door to him and Isabella. Life couldn't get any better.

"You better get Reggie before I bust his ass," Kiki told Taz. They were sitting in Taz's living room, smoking a blunt of loud, while Bella was making D'Azia and Neveah something to eat.

"Ha ha, what he do?" he asked, pulling on the blunt.

"He trying to fuck my twin."

"Oh yeah, tell him that's dead, that's me right there," he said and dodged the remote she threw at him.

"A cute face and a fat ass get y'all every time. Speaking of a fat ass, I seen you and ole girl Nesha the other day too."

"Shhh." He looked towards the kitchen where Isabella was.

Taz and Quanesha had been fucking around on the low. She'd transferred to the University of Miami and Taz had been fucking her brains out ever since.

"That's my little PYT," he bragged.

"How old is that girl?"

"Nineteen."

"A'ight, nigga, them young girls get attached, especially if you sexing her real crazy," Kiki warned.

"Nah, she good. She knows about Isabella. We got an understanding of what we are."

"We going to see." She smirked.

"Enough of that. How everything going in the A?"

Since Taz had put TK in position, he'd done exactly what he said he was going to do and fallen all the way back from the streets. It felt so good not to have to look over his shoulder all the time. Not too many people could say they had did half the shit he'd done and been able to fall all the way back and live happily ever after. It was the type of shit you only read about in books and saw in movies. Taz was just going to sit back, make babies, and get rich. The only time he got involved was when TK asked him for advice, and even then, Taz wasn't really involved. He just told TK what he'd do.

"It's going way better than expected. The profits go up every week and we don't really have to do nothing but drop work off. You know PJ and Reggie still be in the trap from time to time, but other than that it's all good. You can't tell." She rubbed her ears, showing off hands full of rings and diamond studs in her ears.

"What y'all in here talking about?" Isabella asked, sitting in Taz's lap as Kiki rolled her eyes.

Kiki and Bella were cordial, but they were anything but friends. They put up with each other for Taz's sake.

"Damn, nosy," Taz joked. "What my son been doing?" He rubbed her big belly.

Isabella was now seven months pregnant, but she looked nine. They found out she was having a boy, and Taz couldn't have been happier. Taz wanted a son so he could carry his name.

"Whatever, boy. I see I'm not invited to y'all's little pow wow, so I'm going to go finish decorating the baby's room." Bella pouted.

"Bella, shut up, you know you can stay right here." Taz grabbed her hips as she tried to get up.

"No, I'm good. Besides, I need to get it finished before the baby shower."

She pried his hands off and wobbled towards the back.

"She's so dramatic," Kiki said.

"Watch your mouth before I go in it."

"What you want, boy?" Kiki answered her phone. "Yeah, he right here, why you ain't call his phone? Here." She passed Taz the phone.

"Yo."

"Bro, I need to holler at you ASAP, and not over the phone, in person," TK said.

"What's good?" Taz could hear the urgency in his voice.

"Shit crazy. How long before you can get to the A?"

"I'm going to be on the next flight out."

"Bet." He hung up.

"What was that all about?" Kiki asked as he gave her her phone back.

"I don't know, but it's serious. I can hear it in his voice."

Just then the doorbell rang.

"I got it, bae!" Isabella yelled.

"Well, let me get out of here. I need to go work on my tan," said Kiki.

"Shut your stupid ass up. You can't get no darker," he laughed.

Kiki looked over his shoulder and gasped. "What the fuck!"

Taz turned around to find Hector and a mob of his henchmen enter his living room with guns drawn.

"What the fuck y'all got going on?" Taz amped up.

A couple of the henchmen stepped toward Kiki. Taz stepped between them and her as Kiki whipped out her own weapon.

"Y'all got me fucked up! What's up?" she barked.

Hector looked at Taz. "This has nothing to do with you.

She's Marvin and Kiana's daughter Meosha. She's part of their family. Do you remember when I said she looks familiar? I couldn't place her face until a few days ago.

"First off, she's not Meosha. Secondly, what's your beef with them?" asked Taz.

Hector looked from Taz to Kiki with a hardened stare. "Her mother Kiana killed Isabella and Juan's mother," he snarled.

A thick silence enveloped the room.

To Be Continued...
Confessions of a Gangsta 2
Coming Soon

Submission Guideline

Submit the first three chapters of your completed manuscript to ldpsubmissions@gmail.com, subject line: Your book's title. The manuscript must be in a .doc file and sent as an attachment. Document should be in Times New Roman, double spaced and in size 12 font. Also, provide your synopsis and full contact information. If sending multiple submissions, they must each be in a separate email.

Have a story but no way to send it electronically? You can still submit to LDP/Ca$h Presents. Send in the first three chapters, written or typed, of your completed manuscript to:

LDP: Submissions Dept
Po Box 870494
Mesquite, Tx 75187

DO NOT send original manuscript. Must be a duplicate.

Provide your synopsis and a cover letter containing your full contact information.

Thanks for considering LDP and Ca$h Presents.

<u>Coming Soon from Lock Down Publications/Ca$h Presents</u>

BOW DOWN TO MY GANGSTA

By **Ca$h**

TORN BETWEEN TWO

By **Coffee**

BLOOD STAINS OF A SHOTTA **III**

By **Jamaica**

STEADY MOBBIN **III**

By **Marcellus Allen**

BLOOD OF A BOSS **VI**

SHADOWS OF THE GAME II

By **Askari**

LOYAL TO THE GAME **IV**

By **T.J. & Jelissa**

A DOPEBOY'S PRAYER **II**

By **Eddie "Wolf" Lee**

IF LOVING YOU IS WRONG... **III**

By **Jelissa**

TRUE SAVAGE **VII**

MIDNIGHT CARTEL

DOPE BOY MAGIC II

By **Chris Green**

BLAST FOR ME **III**

DUFFLE BAG CARTEL **IV**

HEARTLESS GOON **IV**

A SAVAGE DOPEBOY II

Confessions of a Gangsta

DRUG LORDS III
By **Ghost**
A HUSTLER'S DECEIT III
KILL ZONE **II**
BAE BELONGS TO ME III
SOUL OF A MONSTER III
By **Aryanna**
THE COST OF LOYALTY **III**
By **Kweli**
THE SAVAGE LIFE III
By **J-Blunt**
KING OF NEW YORK V
COKE KINGS IV
BORN HEARTLESS III
By **T.J. Edwards**
GORILLAZ IN THE BAY V
De'Kari
THE STREETS ARE CALLING II
Duquie Wilson
KINGPIN KILLAZ IV
STREET KINGS III
PAID IN BLOOD III
CARTEL KILLAZ IV
Hood Rich
SINS OF A HUSTLA II
ASAD
TRIGGADALE III

211

Nicholas Lock

Elijah R. Freeman
KINGZ OF THE GAME V
Playa Ray
SLAUGHTER GANG IV
RUTHLESS HEART II
By Willie Slaughter
THE HEART OF A SAVAGE II
By Jibril Williams
FUK SHYT II
By Blakk Diamond
THE DOPEMAN'S BODYGAURD II
By Tranay Adams
TRAP GOD II
By Troublesome
YAYO II
A SHOOTER'S AMBITION II
By S. Allen
GHOST MOB
Stilloan Robinson
KINGPIN DREAMS II
By Paper Boi Rari
CREAM
By Yolanda Moore
SON OF A DOPE FIEND II
By Renta
FOREVER GANGSTA II
By Adrian Dulan

Confessions of a Gangsta

LOYALTY AIN'T PROMISED
By Keith Williams
THE PRICE YOU PAY FOR LOVE II
By Destiny Skai
THE LIFE OF A HOOD STAR
By Rashia Wilson
TOE TAGZ II
By Ah'Million
CONFESSIONS OF A GANGSTA II
By Nicholas Lock

Available Now

RESTRAINING ORDER **I & II**
By **CA$H & Coffee**
LOVE KNOWS NO BOUNDARIES **I II & III**
By **Coffee**
RAISED AS A GOON I, II, III & IV
BRED BY THE SLUMS I, II, III
BLAST FOR ME I & II
ROTTEN TO THE CORE I II III
A BRONX TALE I, II, III
DUFFEL BAG CARTEL I II III
HEARTLESS GOON
A SAVAGE DOPEBOY
HEARTLESS GOON I II III
DRUG LORDS I II

Nicholas Lock

By **Ghost**
LAY IT DOWN **I & II**
LAST OF A DYING BREED
BLOOD STAINS OF A SHOTTA I & II
By **Jamaica**
LOYAL TO THE GAME
LOYAL TO THE GAME II
LOYAL TO THE GAME III
LIFE OF SIN I, II III
By **TJ & Jelissa**
BLOODY COMMAS I & II
SKI MASK CARTEL I II & III
KING OF NEW YORK I II,III IV
RISE TO POWER I II III
COKE KINGS I II III
BORN HEARTLESS I II
By **T.J. Edwards**
IF LOVING HIM IS WRONG…I & II
LOVE ME EVEN WHEN IT HURTS I II III
By **Jelissa**
WHEN THE STREETS CLAP BACK I & II III
By **Jibril Williams**
A DISTINGUISHED THUG STOLE MY HEART I II & III
LOVE SHOULDN'T HURT I II III IV
RENEGADE BOYS I II III IV
By **Meesha**
A GANGSTER'S CODE I &, II III

Confessions of a Gangsta

A GANGSTER'S SYN I II III

THE SAVAGE LIFE I II

By J-Blunt

PUSH IT TO THE LIMIT

By **Bre' Hayes**

BLOOD OF A BOSS **I, II, III, IV, V**

SHADOWS OF THE GAME

By **Askari**

THE STREETS BLEED MURDER **I, II & III**

THE HEART OF A GANGSTA I II& III

By **Jerry Jackson**

CUM FOR ME

CUM FOR ME 2

CUM FOR ME 3

CUM FOR ME 4

CUM FOR ME 5

An **LDP Erotica Collaboration**

BRIDE OF A HUSTLA **I II & II**

THE FETTI GIRLS **I, II& III**

CORRUPTED BY A GANGSTA I, II III, IV

BLINDED BY HIS LOVE

THE PRICE YOU PAY FOR LOVE

By **Destiny Skai**

WHEN A GOOD GIRL GOES BAD

By **Adrienne**

THE COST OF LOYALTY I II

By Kweli

Nicholas Lock

A GANGSTER'S REVENGE **I II III & IV**

THE BOSS MAN'S DAUGHTERS

THE BOSS MAN'S DAUGHTERS II

THE BOSSMAN'S DAUGHTERS III

THE BOSSMAN'S DAUGHTERS IV

THE BOSS MAN'S DAUGHTERS **V**

A SAVAGE LOVE **I & II**

BAE BELONGS TO ME I II

A HUSTLER'S DECEIT I, II, III

WHAT BAD BITCHES DO I, II, III

SOUL OF A MONSTER I II

KILL ZONE

By **Aryanna**

A KINGPIN'S AMBITON

A KINGPIN'S AMBITION **II**

I MURDER FOR THE DOUGH

By **Ambitious**

TRUE SAVAGE

TRUE SAVAGE II

TRUE SAVAGE **III**

TRUE SAVAGE **IV**

TRUE SAVAGE **V**

TRUE SAVAGE **VI**

DOPE BOY MAGIC

MIDNIGHT CARTEL

By **Chris Green**

A DOPEBOY'S PRAYER

Confessions of a Gangsta

By **Eddie "Wolf" Lee**

THE KING CARTEL **I, II & III**

By **Frank Gresham**

THESE NIGGAS AIN'T LOYAL **I, II & III**

By **Nikki Tee**

GANGSTA SHYT **I II &III**

By **CATO**

THE ULTIMATE BETRAYAL

By **Phoenix**

BOSS'N UP **I , II & III**

By **Royal Nicole**

I LOVE YOU TO DEATH

By Destiny J

I RIDE FOR MY HITTA

I STILL RIDE FOR MY HITTA

By **Misty Holt**

LOVE & CHASIN' PAPER

By **Qay Crockett**

TO DIE IN VAIN

SINS OF A HUSTLA

By **ASAD**

BROOKLYN HUSTLAZ

By **Boogsy Morina**

BROOKLYN ON LOCK I & II

By **Sonovia**

GANGSTA CITY

By **Teddy Duke**

Nicholas Lock

A DRUG KING AND HIS DIAMOND I & II III
A DOPEMAN'S RICHES
HER MAN, MINE'S TOO I, II
CASH MONEY HO'S
By Nicole Goosby
TRAPHOUSE KING **I II & III**
KINGPIN KILLAZ I II III
STREET KINGS I II
PAID IN BLOOD **I II**
CARTEL KILLAZ I II III
By **Hood Rich**
LIPSTICK KILLAH **I, II, III**
CRIME OF PASSION I II & III
By **Mimi**
STEADY MOBBN' **I, II, III**
By **Marcellus Allen**
WHO SHOT YA **I, II, III**
SON OF A DOPE FIEND
Renta
GORILLAZ IN THE BAY **I II III IV**
DE'KARI
TRIGGADALE I II
Elijah R. Freeman
GOD BLESS THE TRAPPERS I, II, III
THESE SCANDALOUS STREETS I, II, III
FEAR MY GANGSTA I, II, III
THESE STREETS DON'T LOVE NOBODY I, II

Confessions of a Gangsta

BURY ME A G I, II, III, IV, V

A GANGSTA'S EMPIRE I, II, III, IV

THE DOPEMAN'S BODYGAURD

Tranay Adams

THE STREETS ARE CALLING

Duquie Wilson

MARRIED TO A BOSS... I II III

By Destiny Skai & Chris Green

KINGZ OF THE GAME I II III IV

Playa Ray

SLAUGHTER GANG I II III

RUTHLESS HEART

By Willie Slaughter

THE HEART OF A SAVAGE

By Jibril Williams

FUK SHYT

By Blakk Diamond

DON'T F#CK WITH MY HEART I II

By Linnea

ADDICTED TO THE DRAMA I II III

By Jamila

YAYO

A SHOOTER'S AMBITION

By S. Allen

TRAP GOD

By Troublesome

FOREVER GANGSTA

By Adrian Dulan

TOE TAGZ

By Ah'Million

KINGPIN DREAMS

By Paper Boi Rari

CONFESSIONS OF A GANGSTA

By Nicholas Lock

<u>BOOKS BY LDP'S CEO, CA$H</u>

<u>TRUST IN NO MAN</u>

<u>TRUST IN NO MAN 2</u>

<u>TRUST IN NO MAN 3</u>

<u>BONDED BY BLOOD</u>

<u>SHORTY GOT A THUG</u>

<u>THUGS CRY</u>

<u>THUGS CRY 2</u>

<u>THUGS CRY 3</u>

<u>TRUST NO BITCH</u>

<u>TRUST NO BITCH 2</u>

<u>TRUST NO BITCH 3</u>

<u>TIL MY CASKET DROPS</u>

<u>RESTRAINING ORDER</u>

<u>RESTRAINING ORDER 2</u>

<u>IN LOVE WITH A CONVICT</u>

<u>Coming Soon</u>

BONDED BY BLOOD 2

BOW DOWN TO MY GANGSTA

Nicholas Lock